THE BANDAGED RIDERS

In the shambles of the stricken, defeated South, lawless men like Reuben Slatt and his ragged followers roam free. Slatt has an idea: adopt the flag of the victors to forcibly take over a town, bleed the place dry, and shoot as traitors any Southerner who dares raise a hand against them. But there is one man who will not stand by and see people exploited and humbled. And yet he knows nothing about himself — not even for which side he had fought during the war . . .

GORDON LANDSBOROUGH

THE BANDAGED RIDERS

Complete and Unabridged

LINFORD
Leicester

First published in Great Britain in 1954
as *The Bandaged Riders* by Mike M'Cracken

First Linford Edition
published 2016

*A catalogue record for this book is available
from the British Library.*

ISBN 978–1–4448–2683–8

Published by
F. A. Thorpe (Publishing)
Anstey, Leicestershire

Set by Words & Graphics Ltd.
Anstey, Leicestershire
Printed and bound in Great Britain by
T. J. International Ltd., Padstow, Cornwall

This book is printed on acid-free paper

1

Something struck from among the lush green swamp grasses. There was a rustle, a ripple in the water that was dart-shaped. It aimed for the hairy face and gulping lips.

It missed the man's eyes, that old man in the clothes that looked as old as he was. He felt the sharp, poisoned needle-teeth stab into a cheek that was like leather.

The stinging pain of that savage bite pulled his head out of the water, so suddenly that he made a commotion and the water moccasin was lost in the spreading waves.

The old-timer rolled and sat on his haunches on the causeway that led to the world outside the swamps. The water trickled off his wet face and dropped, and was caught gleaming on the scraggy hair of a chest revealed by a dirty and inadequate shirt.

It itched, and he scratched himself, while his faded grey eyes blinked dismally about him. Then he rubbed his cheek.

Two men were standing there. The old-timer lifted a quavering voice. 'That's gonna make me ill,' he said. 'Doggone it, I'll be sicker'n a cow that's bin at mount'in ash berries.'

They didn't speak. They stood together on that green causeway, eyes narrowed against the almost tropical sunshine, and they watched him.

The old man came over on to his knees and then rose stiffly, shoving off from the hot soil with hands seeming too weak to be of help to him. Then he teetered round, and they expected him to drop dead in his tracks, but he just said, vaguely: 'Them things allus do that to me. Doggone 'em, I don't ever think to look out for 'em when I drink.'

One of the two men stirred and detached himself from his companion. In a bemused way the old man realised that this fellow who now moved had been leaning on his shorter, stocky companion. Like a man weak, mebbe hurt.

This galoot was young, with straight fair hair that came dropping down his face in front of his ears, like a ram's horns. He had a thin face, a surprisingly little face on top of a tall, bony form.

He wore store pants and black coat, much like a gambling man, but the pants were stuffed into riding boots as if the galoot did more than sit around a table.

There was a black stain on the fancy-striped shirt under that black gambler's coat. Blood went black like that in a matter of two hours in that drying heat.

The young man spoke, and his voice was incredulous. 'You got bit. We seen it. Bit in the cheek by a water moccasin. Don't they kill people nowadays, them dam' snakes?'

The old-timer had found his hat, a thing that hadn't much crown and had lost some of its brim. He was uneasy, unhappy in the way he looked at those two men. He started to walk deeper into the swamp, and he kept looking over his shoulder at the pair, like a man wanting to be rid of them.

They started to walk after him, their eyes fixed on his scrub-bearded, unhappy old face. There was menace in those eyes, the blue ones of the young man and the sullen brown ones of his companion.

The old man's voice gave an uncertain answer to that query. 'I don't reckon so. Not all the time.' He was so intent on watching the two men who came slowly after him that he crossed his feet and nearly fell. Then a spasm of pain gripped his stomach and he tottered along holding his hand flat across his stomach where it hurt.

Wryly, pain-filled, his voice jerked back: 'Them things don't kill me. Not till now, anyhow. Guess I've gotten kinda used to their pisen. Jes' makes me sick an' sick an' sick. Gonna be mighty sick in a minute, folks, you watch. Doggone, why don't I look for them critters, 'stead of allus pokin' my head in where they are.'

A spasm racked his thin-boned, fleshless frame. His face contorted, and he held his head over a bush. He was sick for long minutes on end.

The two men stood impassively by and watched him, and there was no pity on their faces and no word of compassion on their compressed lips.

When the worst of those agonies was over, the old-timer lifted a face as grey as any living face could go and said, as if with his last strength: 'Gonna . . . lie down. Reckon here's as good as any place else.'

He slumped in the shadow of that bush into which he had emptied his writhing stomach. The fair-haired man's eyes went brittle grey.

'You ain't gonna sleep yet awhiles, pardner,' he rapped, and in that same moment he looked back along the causeway as if fearing to see pursuit.

Then he came forward quickly, his hand reaching roughly towards that sick old man. But the action of bending brought on a vertigo that made him reel and clasp a hand to his injured shoulder. He groaned, and his face went white as the pain hit him all over again.

His companion held him upright above the old man. Brown eyes looked bewildered. Here was not a thinking man. The younger galoot with the straight fair hair gave him orders as he always had to.

'Kick the old devil on to his feet, Tozer. Go on, boot him till he gets up.' His voice was cruel, encouraging brutality — demanding it to satisfy some inner compulsion that wasn't understood by the darker, older man.

But Tozer faithfully followed orders. He kicked the protesting old man on to his feet. Then Tozer looked at the blond galoot and growled: 'Now what?'

'You know the way through this swamp?' the wounded man asked. He was straightening slowly, with infinite care, as if the pain was moving reluctantly out of his torn shoulder muscles.

'Ain't no place through this hyar swamp,' quavered the old man. A pointed tongue licked around toothless lips again. He was feeling desperately sick. 'Jes' paths leadin' slap-bang into the quags.'

'That's good enough.' The blond galoot nodded. 'We don't know 'em. Jes' followed your tracks, an' wouldn't know where to go from here.'

Tozer growled: 'God, I wish I'd got a hoss. Me, I'm tellin' you I don't like this place. Not swamps.' His brown eyes stared with fear and anger into the quaking, bubbling mud just off the causeway. A mist was coming off it, a mist that evaporated into nothingness a foot above the mud because of the sun's heat.

The blond galoot snapped: 'We ain't got no hosses. We ain't got no place to go if we had. Not until this fin's healed.'

'An' then?'

'Then we go out an' git hosses,' said the younger man, and in his tone was concentrated viciousness; in his eyes was distilled hatred. 'We'll have some place to go an' somethin' to do, an' by then there won't be nob'dy out there waitin' to git us.'

He swore under his breath. The old man was watching his face, but his tired brain got no significance from what he saw. Just a feeling that here was a bad galoot, a man to humour if at all possible.

At which moment he bent double again as sickness hit him. The blond galoot didn't let him ride through his sickness this time. He was uneasy about their nearness to the outer world. And it wasn't long since they'd been with their enemies and lost their horses.

He gave the word to Tozer, and Bully Tozer kicked the old man into movement. 'Go on, fellar,' Tozer ordered roughly. 'Into them swamps. Git us hid where nob'dy c'n find us, an' we'll let you sit around all the time an' sick your heart up.'

He grinned at his own crude humour and looked across at the blond galoot. 'That right, eh, Sku?'

Johnny Skulach brought his head whirling round. He wasn't in any mood for humour. He was a wounded man, with all the disadvantages that that implied.

His eyes fixed on the startled Tozer. 'Didn't you hear? Thar's someone outside. C'mon, git the so-an'-so movin'.'

Something like panic seized them both now, and between them they jerked the old-timer into movement. Stumbling, half-blind with the pain that had come from those poisoned fangs, he yet led the way through those stinking, pulsing, moving swamps. This had been home for Old Eb for years now . . .

Back along the causeway a man stirred in the long grasses, his eyes puzzled, watching them go. Then he receded back into the grasses, and all was silent over the swamplands again.

2

Eb was moaning as he staggered along, the poison from that vicious water snake coursing through his veins.

It was true, as old Eb said, that he couldn't be killed by these small snakes. He had been bitten several times in his long life, and his body must have acquired an immunity. All the same, it was painful to be bitten, and right now Eb was a very sick man.

His two companions had no sympathy for him. They were concerned with their own safety, and the suspicion that someone had moved back along the causeway filled them with panic.

They wanted to get deeper into these swamps that seemed so inconsistent on the edge of the prairie cattle lands of north-east Texas.

Tozer growled continuously and in bad temper under his breath as they went along that one solid winding strip of earth between the quagmires. His brown, mean eyes roved constantly from left to right, and then over his shoulder to look behind.

Like Johnny Skulach he carried a Colt on his hip, in a holster that showed signs of much wear.

He walked with his hand on his gun, ready for action, and he growled: 'Stinkin' place. Doggone it, I don't like this place. I like outside. Give me hossflesh an' the open prairie to ride on.'

He was supporting Skulach with his free arm, though Skulach was walking well again, the pain having subsided for the moment. He was more inconvenienced by the stiffness of that wounded shoulder than by actual physical hurt.

It took them a good twenty minutes to come to an island at the end of the causeway. It seemed like an island, anyway. Just a spit of land that lifted just a dozen feet higher than the water and mud that surrounded it.

They saw it through the drooping, moss-hung swamp trees, that seemed to bend long and untidy fingers down towards the warm waters of the swamp.

There was just a fringe of bushes that marked the edge of the dry land, and in the centre of a clearing no more than fifty yards across was a solitary reed-thatched hut made of untidy stick supports interlaced with leafy branches.

It was crude, but this was old Eb's home.

They walked up to the hut, suspiciously, though old Eb quavered that he lived by himself. These men from the plains did not take chances. Someone might be lurking inside that hut.

But when they went through the opening that served as a door, they saw nothing in the interior save for an old blanket that was Eb's bed.

Skulach lowered himself groaning on to the blanket. His face was drained of blood, because of the exertions of the last few hours. His eyes drooped, and all he could say was: 'Get me water, Tozer. Water to drink, and some to get this shirt clean away from the damned blood.'

Bully Tozer stood in the doorway, blocking out the light. A dull-minded, low-thinking man of primitive desires. And yet curiously devoted to this worthless Johnny Skulach whom he followed.

He was trying to think out where he might find the water Skulach needed.

Then he thought of the old man and turned and stumbled out, his eyes narrowing as they met the full force of the torrid noon-day sun. He blinked and looked about him.

He felt oppressed. Hemming him in was the swamp vegetation — those low but closely-pressing swamp trees. They were dark in colour except for the few silvery-leafed willows. That sombreness was somehow depressing and chilling even to a man as insensitive as Bully Tozer.

Or perhaps instinct told him of the

dangers that might be lurking in every square yard of that stinking, fetid swamp.

He saw the old man, like a bundle of rags and bones, huddled into the shadow of the hut. He walked across and stirred him with his toe, without feeling or tenderness or compassion for the sick old man.

Old Eb lifted a grey exhausted face. His tired, pain-dulled eyes flickered open and focused uncertainly upon the head that was silhouetted against the blue Texan sky.

Tozer growled: 'Sku wants water.' His slow mind got around to the thought, and then he added: 'Reckon so do I.'

The old man just stared. Tozer snapped into a fury which was characteristic.

He pulled out his Colt and lifted it threateningly, while he jerked the sick old man into a sitting position. The gun barrel poised a few inches above the old man's forehead, ready to strike him down at the least frustration.

'Goddam, didn't you hear me? Sku wants water, an' so do I. Where d'you keep your water? Is that water fit to drink?'

His head jerked towards the unpleasant-smelling water that showed in patches among the green-slimed mud.

Old Eb shook his head ever so slightly. 'It's salt,' his voice croaked. 'You got to go back to the springs to git fresh water.'

'Along the causeway?' Tozer looked baffled.

Eb nodded.

'Ain't you got no water nearer than that?'

Eb thought, and then said: 'Thar's a can back of the hut. Mebbe I didn't use all that water. I was goin' out for food.'

'Food?' That was something else he and Skulach would have to think about.

But first Sku wanted water. Tozer trudged heavily round to the back. There was some inside an old iron pot.

He took the vessel into the hut. As it

swilled, red rust rose to discolour the water, but it was water, and would do.

He was just stooping to go through that door-opening when both he and Johnny Skulach heard the distant rattle of gunfire.

Skulach came sitting up on that blanket immediately. He was sweating, and his face glistened in the shadowy half-light. There was fear in those blue eyes — the fear of a trapped animal.

Skulach said quickly: 'Hear that? Gun talk!'

Tozer turned to look uneasily back along the causeway. 'Mebbe it was wrong to stick our necks into this place,' he growled. 'Reckon we're like trapped rats.'

Skulach's gun was out, and his eyes were looking through the patch of brightness that was the doorway.

Again they heard the rattle of gunfire, as if a second volley had been dispatched. Now they were able to calculate the distance.

'It's outside,' Skulach muttered, and

his gun lowered. In that stillness, gunfire would carry three or four miles. He figured that the battle, wherever it raged, was a good way out from their hideout.

There was no more firing after that, and in time both relaxed. Thirst demanded attention, and they scooped out water in a small tin panikin and drank.

Then, under the direction of Skulach, Tozer soaked the shirt front and eased it away from the wound. Skulach kept groaning and cursing the man for his clumsiness.

And then he shouted with pain as Tozer lost patience and dragged the bandage off the injury. It opened up and began to bleed.

Skulach knew he had to stand the pain, even so. He rolled over and let Tozer examine his back. The bullet had gone right through his flesh, perhaps chipping bone on the way, but mostly only damaging muscle.

Tozer cleaned up the wound and

bandaged it with strips of shirt. It meant that Skulach would have to get himself a new shirt soon, and there weren't many shirts in that part of the world since the war had ended.

When it was over, Tozer sat against the wall of the hut, and they both relaxed.

But Tozer never took his eyes off that causeway. The more he watched the more he wanted to go on watching, because of the certainty that danger was waiting out there for them.

Skulach felt irritable. He was in pain, and he wanted to pass on some of his discomfort to others.

He said: 'I don't reckon they'll think to come in the quag. They'll figger we struck off towards a town to git hosses. Yeah, I figger we're safe.'

Then Skulach noticed the pangs of hunger, and ordered Tozer out in search of food.

That took him to the sick old man, who had to be kicked into co-operative consciousness again.

‘Food?’ It took the old man minutes even to think of the meaning of the word.

Then his voice quavered. ‘I ain’t got none. I was tellin’ you, I was a-going out to rustle up some grub when I met you.’

Tozer walked back to report. ‘He ain’t got no food.’

The news made Sku nasty. He came rearing up again on that blanket, his lank blond hair stringing across his face, surrounding his glittering grey eyes.

He shouted at Tozer. ‘Holy cow, don’t stand there an’ say we ain’t got food. How in hell do we live here without it?’

Tozer stood there as impassively as a Texan longhorn bull. Just as brutish and just as unreceptive to the anger and harsh words of his companion.

Men had marvelled at it before. Tozer, who would take no insult from any other man, never seemed to notice them from his chosen trail companion, Johnny Skulach.

Johnny was feeling the heat and the biting of those insects. He was sore and frustrated by this enforced hiding in this evil-smelling place. He was vicious, accordingly, and wanted to take it out on someone.

'You gotta get food, see? Go on, you goldarn mule-head, and find some grub. You should have thought about it afore.'

Which was a bit hard on Tozer. But Skulach's anger drove the smaller, thicker-set man shambling out round the hut again.

A third time old Eb found himself jerked from a pain-ridden doze into an even more painful consciousness. A big hand grasped his torn old shirt around the chest, and his startled eyes fluttered open to see Tozer's angry, blue-chinned face within inches of his own.

Tozer was already working himself into anger. As he shook the helpless old man, he growled: 'Food! D'you hear me, you old devil, we want food. Ef you don't rustle up grub pronto I'll bust that old skull of yourn!'

Eb's dull eyes could see the threat of that raised Colt. He could understand the danger that threatened him; yet there was little he could do. He was too weak to move, and anyway there just wasn't food within miles of them.

Tozer's fury spilled over. 'Blast you, you won't even speak, huh?'

He lifted his gun a few more inches preparatory to that savage, slashing blow that would split the old man's head open. It was the kind of thing that Bully Tozer had done before and liked doing. All he had to do was work himself into a suitable rage and he could do things like that.

The gun began its brutal downward course.

But it never reached its target. Even before gun barrel met that defenceless, balding old head, something happened to jerk Tozer's sadistic attention away from old Eb.

A girl screamed within a hundred yards of them.

3

Skulach was at the door, gun in hand, even as Tozer blundered round the corner of the hut.

Skulach shouted: 'You heard that? A gal! What's a gal doin' here?'

And then he shut his mouth. Panic had made him shout. Self-preservation quietened him now.

No death crept towards them, though. Instead, a girl came running blunderingly, blind almost with terror, out from the screening swamp trees and lush green reeds and grasses. She came flying into the open glade, her head turned to look in terror back the way she had come. She was almost up to the hut when her face slewed round and looked at them.

When she saw men standing there, her immediate reaction was relief.

She stumbled right between them.

Then she turned, facing that causeway behind their forms as if she thought they would protect her. They could hear the quick panting of her lungs. It was more than exertion that made her breathe like that, they knew. It was stark terror.

The girl had had an experience just out there along the causeway that had shocked her out of her senses for the moment. But now she was quietening. She was even looking at those two men quickly, with eyes that were calculating and knew the estimate of men's worth.

She had a face that might have been pretty. But there was something about it — a heaviness of expression, a sullenness that was habitual there, and it was not pleasing.

But her hair was good — corn-yellow and long over her shoulder. She wore a shirt that was much patched, and bib-and-brace coverall. On her feet were old boots that clearly hadn't been made for a girl.

She was attractive because of her

youth, and in spite of her unprepossessing clothing and that discontented expression on her face. And Skulach was already noticing it, and thinking about her, and getting ideas into his head.

That was always Johnny Skulach.

Tozer grabbed the girl roughly by the arm. She cried out in pain. She saw his brutal, black-scrubbed face, with its narrowed brown eyes that looked filled with dirt and unpleasantness.

She exclaimed: 'You're hurting!'

Tozer growled: 'I'll hurt a lot more. What are you doin' here? How come you screamed an' came in a-runnin'?'

That brought her thoughts back to the shock she had had. They saw her lick her lips, and her eyes flickered fearfully along the causeway to where it disappeared into the vegetation.

'I was coming along the causeway. I didn't see anything. Then something reached out and grabbed my ankle.'

'Grabbed?' Skulach's fearful eyes jumped to meet those of Tozer. Both their heads swung back immediately to look toward the causeway. Two guns were pointing instantly.

'I looked down. All I saw was a hand. Just a hand, nothing else.'

The girl was shivering in terror, remembering that hand that seemed disembodied because of the grasses that must have hidden the arm and body of the owner.

'I dragged my foot away.' She was panting. 'And then I screamed and began to run.'

Her eyes looked from one man to the other, but they weren't looking at her. She was fast recovering now, and she was thinking hard.

Tozer took a plunging step forward. 'Thar's a fellar out there!'

Skulach snarled. 'Rout him out, Bully. Go on, git the fellar off this swamp, or stick a bullet through his head. Go on, Bully!'

It was like setting a dog on to an intruder, the way Skulach gave orders to that brutish Tozer. And like a dog sicked on to an enemy, Bully Tozer went plunging across the opening to where the girl had appeared. He was a man too low in mentality to entertain any great fears.

The girl and Skulach watched him go at a half-run in among the trees and bushes. They waited, expecting him to open fire, but nothing happened. A good twenty minutes passed, and then, when they were beginning to feel uneasy, Tozer reappeared.

He was carrying a gunny sack. As he shambled across, he shook his head.

'Ain't nobody there,' he growled, joining them. 'Leastways, I didn't find nobody.' He spat, and then wiped away the drool from his chin with the back of his hand.

'I found the place where the galoot had been lyin' up alongside the track. I found this there.' He hefted the filled gunny sack. 'That must have bin the place where he tried to catch her.'

Skulach rapped: 'You followed his tracks?'

'Yeah. He went out at a run, I guess.'

Skulach considered. He was thinking of that gunfire in the world outside. He could guess whose guns had blasted a few lives into eternity in those salvoes. And he was trying to connect this mysterious intruder of the swamps with his enemies outside.

Then his eyes fell on the gunny sack. Tozer interpreted the look and grinned triumphantly. 'We won't go hungry now,' he exclaimed with satisfaction. 'See!'

He tipped the sack and the contents fell out. Nothing very appetising, but food. A hunk of meat. Some flat unleavened corn bread. Some mealies, and some dried beans.

Skulach grunted: 'It'll do. Better git some food made right pronto.'

That was an order, though given to no one specifically. He tore off a hunk of bread and began to eat it, and that brought the girl standing before him.

Her rather heavy-lidded eyes made her look malevolent. She exclaimed:

'That's my bread, mister. You didn't ask.'

Skulach dropped his eyes, so that he was studying her figure. The expression was insolent.

'I don't ask,' he drawled. 'I take.'

He went on eating, and his manner was a challenge. The girl knew it. She also knew she'd get no change from this pair. She accordingly turned away, her figure expressing indignation and suppressed fury.

A groan attracted her attention. She saw movement, and there was old Eb trying to find comfort on that hard ground for his old bones. She knew him.

'Eb!' she said. 'I didn't know you had — guests.' Her voice was sarcastic. She let her eyes trail back to the pair, and then she walked across to old Eb.

There was little kindness on that curiously heavy, discontented young face as she looked down at the worn old man. Her voice, musical because it was young, yet had a rough quality about it as she said: 'You got yourself hurt, old-timer?'

Eb knew that voice. His eyes fixed upon her, though there was no welcome in his expression. He just looked, that was all.

Laconically he said: 'Snake did it. Up an' bit me while I was drinkin'.'

'Again?'

He said sorrowfully: 'Again. Reckon I don't learn quick, do I?'

Then he partly sat up, interested by a thought. 'You're Beth Adie.' It was a flat statement.

She nodded, but now her eyes were trained round to meet those of the lean, blond young man who was wolfing the bread. Bully Tozer was preparing a fire.

Old Eb said, almost as if explaining to himself: 'You come from that farm out there.' His head jerked in the direction of the outer world, roughly that place where they had so recently heard gunfire.

Johnny Skulach came ambling nearer, his hard blue eyes watching the girl intently. Skulach spoke with a mouth stuffed full of bread, so that crumbs stuck to the stubble on his chin.

'You come here often?' She dropped her eyes before his and shook her head sullenly, in the manner of one who resents being questioned. 'How come you came right now, then?'

Hatred blazed in the girl's blue eyes, and while the emotion was with her she looked quite handsome. She said: 'I had to run for it. When they came, my Paw said I'd got to keep out of the way. They was that kind of fellar.'

Johnny stopped eating. 'They?'

Two more strides, the crust of the loaf swinging at his side now, while he took the girl roughly by the shirt and hoisted her round to face him. She cried out in pain as his fingers gripped into her soft flesh underneath that thin cotton shirt.

'Who's they? Who made you run for it?'

Anger flooded over the girl. Her face

went red with fury. She brought both hands up and tore away that grip on her shoulder, digging her nails in to help her. Anger sparked into those blue eyes of Johnny Skulach at that, and for a second it looked as if he might come in with his hand swinging to hit the girl.

But she went back a few yards, panting and facing him. She spat out an explanation, and, because after all his most immediate concern was to know what had gone on out 'there,' he held his temper.

'They came down this mornin'. About a dozen of them.' Now she really spat her words. 'No-goods. Work shys. Hoodlums and scum!'

'What happened?'

Tozer was looking up from his kindling now. He was interested, too. For his life was also at stake.

Beth Adie took a breath and told them. She had been working in the kitchen, preparing food for the return of the men. There wasn't much food, but then there weren't many men now.

Once they'd had the makings of a good farm — mostly ranching on the western slopes of this range to the north of the swamp, but the war had broken their plans. They'd been lucky even to hide away a few beeves in remote gullies beyond reach of Confederate and Yankee hunters these past few years. Now they were just beginning to breed them up and stock their range again.

Meanwhile, there was little meat for them, and only vegetable produce off the land, and little of that to eat.

Her father had reached for his rifle as soon as he saw that scarecrow mob riding over the horizon towards them. The land was filled with roaming bunches of desperadoes who were little more than brigands. Many were deserters from the armies engaged in the war, ended but a bare four months ago, their hands turned against everyone in consequence.

She heard her father muttering as he went out on to the unbleached verandah: 'Wish some of them boys was back.'

There were a dozen in this party, and he was the only man at home. She had caught up an old single-shot Henry, and stood beside him, until he noticed her and ordered her out of sight.

'These hyar varmints is on the look-out for gals like you,' he growled. 'You keep out o' sight, Beth, an' if you see trouble, sneak out the back way an' hide yourself in the quags.'

Reluctantly she had obeyed and gone and hidden in a back room. Reluctant, because there was little in Beth Adie that made her want to obey any man. Life had been hard on this ranch, with little time for the joys that youth should have.

Her father was a man not unkind in motive, but he did not understand the needs of a young girl, who had to be mistress of the ranch since her mother died. He made her work like a man, and there was no softness, no finery, and little pleasure in her workaday existence.

So she had grown up to hate this part of the world, to loathe the existence here on the edge of the cattle country. Her dislike extended to the men whom she knew — men with whom she was not allowed to keep company. They were too old, most of them, anyway; men who had stayed behind when the younger bloods had rallied to the Confederate cause . . .

The scarecrow mob had ridden in, taut in their saddles as their eyes looked around, suspicious of danger. They had relaxed at sight of one old man facing them. Had swung down as if they owned the place.

And in a few minutes they had.

'They just kinda took over,' said Beth furiously, her nails digging into her hands as she clenched her fists in her passion. 'They shoved my father aside and got food and drink, and took what they wanted.'

'Your father had a gun?' That was Johnny Skulach.

‘He couldn’t use it agen a dozen men, could he?’ she blazed. ‘They took it off him, and sent him spinning when he argued.’

The last she’d seen of her father, he’d been sitting on a box just outside on the verandah, his head in his hands like a man who has suffered the last and cruellest blow of all.

‘You got out the back way?’

She nodded sullenly. ‘I figgered they was goin’ to stay there some time, so I put food into a sack an’ crept out the back way.’

Billy Tozer sighed, and fumbled for a match. ‘Wish you’d come ridin’ in on a hoss,’ he said wistfully.

She snapped at him. ‘We didn’t have no hosses. Ef we’d had hosses we’d have been out ahead of that mob.’

Horses were scarce in that part of the country since the Civil War. The few they owned were in use with their hands that day, without so much as a mount spare and in reserve in the stables.

'But that firin'?'

'I got right to the edge of the quags.' Those blue eyes were brooding and bitter, remembering. She was thinking of what she had seen, looking back.

The boys were riding in with a roped steer. Maybe that steer wasn't good for anything but killing, and the meat would have been good.

She'd seen them riding innocently up to the ranch, five men, all unknowing of the danger within the compound.

'I couldn't warn them. They were too far away. I could only stand there and watch and guess what would happen. They were mighty mean men, them fellars.'

The four cowboys had turned to the high gate in the mud-walled compound that had been built in Spanish days. Their presence had been noticed. When the cowboys came into that compound they saw a dozen men with guns covering them.

'Someone fired, and then everybody started firing. I thought they'd all been killed, because they all came down off their hosses.'

Then the smoke had cleared, drifting as if reluctantly away from the scene of the carnage.

'But Jim Willis must have been foxing. Suddenly they saw him runnin', stooped as low as he could go. He took a jump for a hoss, an' tried to fight it out from the saddle. But they got him afore he could get the hoss's head round to face open country. They all up an' fired and got poor Jim in the back.'

There was silence after that, and then the girl's curious glance lifted to meet Johnny Skulach's eyes. Deliberately, offensively, she said: 'They looked like they could be friends of yourn, them fellars.'

Johnny Skulach lifted his hand and hit her across the face, and sent her reeling against the wall of the hut. She didn't cry out, though. She sank crouching against the hut, her face white except for the imprint of his hand on her cheek. But her eyes were brilliant with anger — brilliant with hatred and shock.

Tozer had witnessed the action. His sole comment was a hissing stream of spittle that passed into the fire to one side of his cooking pot. One blow like that, even directed at a woman, made no difference in Billy Tozer's life.

Johnny Skulach hoisted up his pants with his one sound hand. Arrogantly he said: 'I don't take that talk from nobody, see? You hold that tongue of yours still or it'll be so much the worse for you!'

Then he wheeled upon the old man. 'You know the way through these hyar swamps. So does she. How many more folk know about it?'

The old man opened his mouth, then closed it to think. Beth Adie spoke for him, perhaps trying to shield the sick old man from the attentions of the ruffians.

'Quite a few know about it. Kids do, anyway. Lots of 'em. Kids allus come explorin' the quags, I guess. But grown folk don't come in,' she said disdainfully. 'It ain't no place for anyone 'cept people like Eb, wanting to hide.'

'But kids grow up.' There was unease and flickering doubt in those grey eyes. Johnny Skulach had intelligence, and that gave him imagination, and imagination brought terrors. He could visualise things happening long before the event. 'Mebbe quite a few grown-ups around hyar got to know this place when they were kids.'

'That's what I said.' There was complacency in the girl's tone. 'I told you lots of folk know about these paths. But they won't be comin' in. An' your friends won't know the way in, so you can quit worryin'.'

The last words were uttered quickly, fiercely, remembering the vicious blow that had hurt her dignity as much as her flesh. Her eyes blazed, and then she shrank back as Skulach looked at her, and there was no tenderness in that glance, only a warning and threat combined.

But there was something that Skulach wanted to know.

'Them fellars — ?'

Beth looked at him sullenly. She wouldn't speak until he detailed his question more closely.

'What were they like? The fellar that led them?'

Beth tried not to answer, purely out of awkwardness, but then she thought better of it. 'He wasn't so big an' he wasn't so small. He rode his horse like a sailor,' she said. That was the rancher's daughter speaking.

'He wasn't so young, either, and he had the kind of face I don't like to see on a man. Kind of red and squashed up, and with black whiskers all over it. And he was ready to laugh at the least thing. Like when he knocked my father down,' she bit off unpleasantly.

'That,' said Johnny Skulach, 'was Reuben Slatt.' His tone was, if anything, several degrees more vicious than Beth's.

'Slatt?' Beth was startled.

'You've heard of Reuben Slatt?'

'From here to the Mississippi everyone's heard of Reuben Slatt,' Beth said, and she turned away quickly. Slatt had become notorious in the latter part of the war. While the young Confederates were fighting desperately in other fields, Slatt and his ruffians had preyed upon the defenceless old folks back home. He hadn't a name that was enjoyed.

Beth said: 'I reckon when some of those Confederates get out of jail they'll get Reuben Slatt, and they'll take out of him all that he's taken out of their folk while they've been away.' Her manner said that she approved of it, and only wished that the time would come quickly.

Bully Tozer had drifted into the group, crudely wiping his big hands on the seat of his worn, soiled pants. He'd got some meat chopped up, with water and beans, and set them on a pot over the fire. The beans weren't going to be so good, but if they were too hard they could be left soaking for the next meal.

Now he said: 'Reckon it surprised you, gal, to find Slatt ridin' in this county.'

But John Skulach broke in on his companion's grinning words. There were things he wanted to know. 'Was Slatt all right? I mean, was he wounded at all?'

Beth Adie shook her head. Johnny Skulach cursed; then he turned and walked away. They watched him as he stood at a distance, close by a log. He was beside himself with fury.

He took another stride along the edge of the swamp, stamping his feet in fury, again like that petulant child he had once been and still was.

That log moved. There was a swift rush, a sliding motion, and the waters closed over it.

4

For a couple of seconds Johnny Skulach stood there, crouching, just caught off-balance before taking another stride. Then he came back at a quick run to where the others were grouped round the hut. His face was white.

'You saw that? Goddam, I almost trod on it.'

Unexpectedly the old man's voice rose in explanation: 'That was a swamp 'gator. They don't bite — much.'

Skulach looked at him venomously. He had been shaken by the suddenness with which that 'log' had come to life. He was shaken, and yet ashamed to be seen behaving in a cowardly manner.

'Shut your yappin' old mouth,' he snapped viciously. 'Why didn't you tell me they'd got 'gators in this hyar swamp?'

Beth said, nastily: 'I guess they've got

’gators in every swamp within two hundred miles of the Mississippi. You should have known.’

These weren’t men used to such reptiles, and Tozer was licking his lips and letting his eyes dart about from place to place. He breathed quickly. ‘Heck, you don’t mean to say that place is full of ’em?’

Johnny Skulach had something else on his mind. ‘Do they come out at night?’

They knew what he was thinking. They were going to spend this night on this island in the middle of the swamp. What if at night the alligators overran the place? It shattered his nerves to think of it.

But old Eb wasn’t worried by ’gators. He was a little better, too, it seemed, and now he spoke up almost chirpily.

‘Yep, I reckon they come out. But I’ve never had trouble with ’em, mebbe ’cause I allus sleeps with a fire across the doorway.’

Johnny licked his lips. ‘Ef we stay

here tonight we're gonna have the biggest, darndest fire you've ever seen, brother,' he rasped.

His next action was to send Tozer out looking for dry wood, ready for the evening's shadows.

It was too hot for much action, though, and the party retired into the shadows for an uneasy rest. Tozer lay across the front of the hut, his eyes never leaving the causeway that ran into the steaming swamp. Skulach started off by watching the causeway, and ended by looking at Beth Adie instead.

Beth went and lay near to old Eb, as if seeking in his company some sort of protection.

Eb dozed most of the afternoon, with his toothless mouth open, looking at times more like a corpse than a man. Before dusk, though, he seemed to get better, probably revived by his sleep.

Skulach asked harshly: 'Why in God's name do you live here among these 'gators an' water snakes?'

Old Eb sat on his heels and stared

round in perplexity, as if looking at the place for the first time.

Then he sighed. 'I figger most times there ain't nobody here to kick me around,' he said tiredly. 'Out there it allus happens.'

He wiped the moisture away from his hairy chin with trembling fingers.

'Out there everyone carries guns. I figger when men carry guns they kinda like to loose 'em off, an' then someone gets hurt. I sure get hurt enough without stopping lead.'

'Skeered, eh?' That was Bully Tozer jeering and laughing. His brown, almost black eyes smeared the old man with contempt.

Beth Adie said unpleasantly, 'What if he is skeered? Mebbe if some of you fellars weren't so young you wouldn't have such fine talk, either. Old Eb's harmless. He likes to loaf out of the way of armies and battles an' ranchers' feudin'. I don't blame him.'

Those last words were quick, and again held that lilt of viciousness. Beth

Adie was single-minded in her hatred of menfolk and their doings, it seemed.

Skulach seemed about to rise, as if taking affront at the way she spoke to him, but then he thought better of it. The sun was in the west now, but its rays still held heat. He kept back in the shadows and just cursed the heat and rubbed the sweat off his forehead. Something bit him painfully on the neck, and he slapped out and hit nothing.

'Goddam, I ain't stayin' in this place any longer than I need to,' he swore.

Tozer said: 'Let's git now.' His eyes looked to where he had last seen that alligator.

Johnny Skulach said, shaking his head: 'Nope. We cain't git far on foot, an' the only horses we might rustle belong to Reuben Slatt's boys.'

He looked meaningfully at Tozer.

'You wouldn't like to try'n pinch any of Reuben Slatt's hosses, now would you?'

There was fear in Bully Tozer's eyes.

He shook his head and licked his lips. 'I wouldn't try to git his hossflesh for all the silver in Mexico!'

Beth Adie was watching them and listening. There wasn't much that sullen-faced girl missed. She had courage, too, and suddenly she asked: 'Was it Reuben Slatt who drilled that shoulder of yourn?'

Skulach's eyes flickered hatred at the question. He turned his face away. The question was unanswered, but Beth Adie knew the truth, all the same.

It seemed to fill her with some satisfaction, and she was almost smiling as she went across to the fire and looked at the pot boiling away. She went to pick up some more small kindling, but at once Skulach's voice rang out.

'Ef you get any ideas into that purty head about runnin' away from us, forgit 'em. My gun says you won't get off that causeway alive.'

She seemed undaunted by the brutal threat. 'You don't need to worry. I ain't goin' out there while Reuben Slatt's men are in the district. I reckon there's twelve mean hombres out there and only two here!'

Skulach said: 'Tozer, if she opens up that lip to me again like that, go an' knock her down!'

Tozer merely nodded.

Beth Adie tossed her head, but was careful all the same not to say anything further to antagonise that blond, lean young desperado.

Some time later, when evening was close upon them, they ate an unsatisfactory meal. Three of them clustered round the pot and dipped in bread and pulled out meat. The girl competed on even terms with the men, prepared to struggle a little to get her share of food.

Old Eb didn't want any food, or if he did he hadn't the strength or will to crawl over and get any. He just lay in the shadow. He had relapsed again, and seemed more dead than alive. But the others took no notice of him, not even the girl.

The food filled their bellies, at least, and it put Johnny Skulach in a good mood. He was even inclined to be sporty with Beth, putting his hand on her bare arm until she dragged it hurriedly, angrily, away from him.

With the coming of dusk Johnny Skulach started to order the making of a big fire.

Beth Adie watched Tozer shamble around and pile brush and small broken branches a dozen feet away in the door of the reed hut. Then he went across to the little cooking fire to get a burning brand.

Tozer paused on his way back, the burning brand flaming as he held it away from his body. Tozer's eyes were speculative, gauging the height of that fire-to-be and then looking towards the stunted swamp trees that grew out of the mud and water about them.

'Mebbe Slatt will see this fire an' know where we are.'

Skulach hadn't thought of that. He looked into the mist that was already beginning to rise a yard high among those trees, making them appear to swim suspended in space. An unreal, ghostly sight that made a fire all the more imperative.

Beth Adie said: 'They won't see the fire. I've never seen old Eb's fire yet. I reckon these trees are higher than they look.'

It was reassuring. Tozer shambled forward and thrust the branch into the fire, and in a few minutes it was blazing merrily and spreading a bright glow over the darkening glade.

The heat was unpleasant right then. The earth was still warm from the hot day's sun, and they shrank back from the leaping flames and wished for the cooler night wind.

But there was no wind that night. Just stillness over the swamplands, and a silence broken only by the unmusical croak of ten thousand mating bull-frogs.

They grouped about the front of the hut. Eb lying to one side where he had been all the time. Beth Adie sitting by Eb's worn old boots. The other two smoking in the doorway, watching the flame most of the time as if feeling that with the darkness they were safe from pursuit into those treacherous quagmires.

In fact Skulach became too sure he was safe. His fear of the day melted from him like snow before the heat of that fire. In its place came the old Johnny Skulach — a mood of aggression, of cocksureness.

He looked at Beth Adie boldly. Whenever her eyes lifted broodily from the ground to meet his, they were filled with mocking lights of admiration. It was the habitual expression of the gay dog intent on courting. And Johnny Skulach had been a gay dog in his time and was skilled in the arts of making advances — to a certain kind of woman.

Beth Adie did not consider herself that kind, and her lips compressed and those sullen features grew even more sullen as she saw the way his thoughts were going.

She avoided looking at him after a while. Johnny Skulach waited impatiently for a resumption of this courtship by eyes, but then he realised that the girl wasn't playing and he grew angry. Suddenly he rose and went across to her.

She got up at sight of him and moved quickly, catlike toward the darkness.

He jumped and caught her. She found her wrist suddenly grabbed and his clutch was deliberately ungentle. She looked up into a bold face, the face of the arrogant, hunting male. She was frightened but tried to hide it under a storm of anger.

'Let me go! Blast you, take your filthy hands off me!'

'Blast you? That's fine talk from a gal,' he said contemptuously. 'Reckon you've been brung up rough.'

She struggled. He held on to her. His anger was rising as it always did at opposition to his desires.

'I've been brung up rough, too,' he said unpleasantly. 'You've made a mistake, gal. Fightin' me ain't no good. I'm Johnny Skulach, an' I get what I want. You should have bin friendlier and then we'd have got on fine together.'

He reached out with his other hand, the arm that had been hurt that day. But there was still plenty of use in it and he gripped the girl and pulled her towards him. She looked into his eyes and saw there no mercy at all for her. She might just as well have stayed among Reuben Slatt's men for all the good her running away had done her. She knew it and was terrified.

She looked beyond Skulach. Eb had rolled on his side and was watching her. She caught the gleam where the firelight touched his partly-open eyes. But Eb was making no move towards helping her.

Bully Tozer was drawing on his cigarette, watching them without expression on his scrub-covered brutal face.

Desperately the girl called: 'He's hurting me! Don't let him hurt me. Help me — *please!*' In her weakness and fear the proud, sullen girl was reduced to pleading for help.

Eb never moved. Tozer took his cigarette out of his mouth, blew a long stream of smoke down his nostrils, and then resumed his smoking.

Johnny Skulach's triumph was all the more at this demonstration of his power over his two companions. He held her, hurting her, while he threw back his blond head, that curiously small head on that tall bony frame, and laughed uproariously. He was like a cat tormenting a mouse.

She tried to struggle. He was telling her: 'You can forget *them*. Tozer does what I tell him, an' that old fellar had better look out if he thinks to interfere. Now, how about bein' sensible?'

She fought against him, but with his one good arm alone he was able to hold her. He took hold of her hair behind her back and dragged down upon it, so that her face was lifted to his, her lips parted in the agony of that hold upon her head.

Skulach kissed her. It was an unpleasant, ugly brutal kiss that bruised her lips. She spat when he had finished, as if to get rid of the uncleanness of his defiling touch. It was inelegant from a girl, but it was effective.

Skulach jerked his head back to escape that sudden cat-like spitting. It gave Beth her chance. Deliberately, as brutally as he had behaved, she drove her fist into the wound on his shoulder.

Skulach cried out with pain. She saw his mouth open; that face with its frame of blond lank hair contorted in agony.

His grip relaxed for just a second, and she twisted and started to get away.

But she had hurt Skulach. That was something. People didn't hurt Johnny Skulach, neither men nor women, and not regret it.

Skulach shouted in pain, cursing the girl. His long legs took him leaping after her fleeing, frightened form. In that moment neither had a thought for lurking alligators that might have come up on to the bank out of the stinking waters. Neither even saw the black shadows of night that rushed up to meet them.

Tozer and old Eb watched the swift, short pursuit from their positions by the hut, and neither moved and neither changed their expression of indifference.

The girl was on her own.

Skulach caught her. It was inadvertent. She was fleeing just beyond his grasp, instinctively keeping to the dryway that was above water. Another few yards and she'd be completely lost in darkness.

But Skulach fell unexpectedly. Something got between his legs and he tripped, and as he fell instinctively his hand reached out and caught the girl round the ankle. She fell too.

She was sobbing in the darkness, terrified of those next moments in the hands of this brutal young man. She was even crying for mercy, appealing to a softness in his nature that she knew didn't exist.

And Skulach was holding on to her ankle, cursing because he was still in pain and because he didn't like to go stumbling around in the darkness after any girl. He was clawing himself on to his feet, dragging back on that ankle to pull the girl into his grasp. Here it was very dark . . .

A boot stepped out of the darkness on to that outstretched hand. Johnny Skulach screamed with terror, an innate cowardice surfacing immediately at the unexpectedness of that happening.

5

Tozer came leaping to his feet at the fire, his cigarette dropping in a cascade of sparks down his rising form. His hand leapt for his gun and it came out in a crescenting arc of reflected light. It was pointing towards the darkness where dim shadows only could be seen.

Skulach looked up. Against the night's blackness stood a giant's dim form.

Skulach screamed again as the weight of that big, dimly-seen figure pressed upon his hand to make him release his hold about the girl's ankle. He let go.

Skulach was a great fighter behind a dark corner or when his enemy was considerably outnumbered. But that sudden intervention on the part of this unknown man in the darkness shattered his nerve.

Beth scrambled to her feet, her

breath coming quickly because she too had been shocked by the sudden appearance of this stranger.

For one moment there was almost a tableau there on the edge of the firelight. Three figures not moving, hardly to be seen, waiting for action on the part of the other.

Bully Tozer supplied it. He was lurching across, trying to distinguish one form from another. His gun was pointing, trying to aim upon the man who had made his pardner scream.

Then this stranger from the blackness of the swamp spoke. It was a voice that was rock hard and yet there was no uncouth, rasping quality about it. The kind of voice that might go with a pleasant personality, the girl thought.

'Put that gun down. Fire that gun an' you'll bring the whole blamed pack of Slatt's men into the swamps!'

Both Skulach, crouching at his feet, and Beth Adie, shrinking away, saw the gesture from the tall stranger's head as he indicated ‘outside.’

‘Thar’s some of ’em bivvied right on the edge of the quags right now!’

Tozer didn’t think fast. He wasn’t going to put his gun down just because someone talked him out of shooting, anyway. He was bunching forward, snarling, his gun swinging round to cover that speaker. Skulach in panic shouted from the ground: ‘Hold up, Tozer. Blast you. Listen to what he says. We don’t want Slatt’s mob to know we’re in the quags.’

Skulach pulled his hand away and the stranger permitted the action. Then the blond young desperado staggered to his feet. Beth Adie came with a sudden run up to the side of the stranger, yet she wasn’t sure of her actions and held back a couple of feet while she tried to make out his face in the darkness.

The stranger ignored them all. He just brushed past Bully Tozer and headed for the fire. They followed him in a line, the girl last. They saw a tall, lean young man, big but not as big as the darkness had made him appear a few moments ago.

They saw him walk resolutely to where the cooking pot stood, and he squatted on his heels and fingered in the stew for meat. There wasn't much left but the beans had gone soft and he scooped some up and ate them avidly. He saw the last of the bread and chased up the stew with it and ate all the while as if without the slightest concern for an audience.

It gave Skulach time to get his nerve back again. He pulled himself together. His vicious little brain was thinking: 'I got to square things. I ain't gonna let no guy make a fool of me in front of Tozer an' this gal!'

Pride was a great thing with Skulach. He had to be top dog in everything. Now the rage welled up within him and he gripped his gun as he stood behind that squatting figure.

Old Eb came to life. He'd been watching from back beyond the fire. Everyone had dismissed him as of no consequence but now he asserted himself.

'I wouldn't sit with my back to that skunk, brother,' the quavering old voice said. 'Reckon he's gonna draw a gun on you jes' to settle your hash fer standin' on his pretty paw.'

Probably that hungry stranger had guessed what was going on behind his back and didn't need the warning. But he did at least rise at the old man's words, holding that iron pot by the rim. He turned. It was the first time they'd seen his face.

Just a face. Not good-looking, not unpleasant to look at. Well muscled, but too gaunt, as if he had lived without overmuch food in the past weeks.

He had a beard that was clipped almost skin-tight, which told of a lack of razor. He was wearing a ragged old coat such as sheepherders wear on winter's nights. A shirt open almost down to his belt for lack of buttons. Drab grey pants and boots that weren't usually seen in cattle country.

He stood there, legs braced back, challenging the two gunmen with eyes that were pinpoints of light under thick eyebrows.

Skulach wanted trouble. He had Bully Tozer by his side now. He snarled: 'You stood on my hand.'

The stranger said: 'You were maulin' a gal.'

'The hell!' Skulach's temper was inflamed. 'She ain't your gal. I c'n do what I like without your interference!'

'Yeah?' That was all the stranger said.

'Yeah.'

Beth Adie, standing by the old man against the hut, caught her breath quickly, sensing what was to come.

Skulach suddenly drew his gun. But he wasn't going to use it in any normal manner. He leapt in, that wicked barrel raking down to lash open the stranger's face. At the same time Skulach shouted: 'Into him, Bully. Kick the livin' hell out of him!'

Skulach went down with a crash. That tall stranger had swung the iron pot and beaten through Skulach's guard and hit him on the skull. That was Skulach out. Right out!

Tozer came in like a bull that had been tormented by hot irons. He was raving at sight of Johnny Skulach crashing down into unconsciousness. At that moment Tozer was completely mad, and it was something to make this stranger wonder at later.

Yet even so Tozer did not use his gun. Skulach had said don't use it for fear of the men outside. Even with Skulach unconscious, Tozer still followed instructions.

But he came in, gun swinging, trying to catch the stranger off guard — and succeeding.

The two men's forms crashed together. They gripped, holding each other's weapon arm. For a second they stood braced against each other, glaring into each other's face.

Then the stranger kicked Tozer's feet from under him and both crashed to the ground. Tozer fought like a madman. He held on to the stranger and got into him with his knees and feet.

The stranger grunted and lashed out on the ground. But Tozer was pulling him close, and the blows weren't too painful.

They started to roll, the stranger trying to pull away and get to his feet and Tozer intent on holding him. Tozer had lost his gun. Both hands tried to claw into the stranger's face, tried to find his eyeballs.

Desperately the stranger jerked his head back and tried to keep away from those stubby, searching fingers. They were creeping up his face, and then the stranger jabbed with his two palms under Tozer's chin and nearly broke his neck for him.

They staggered to their feet, closed instantly and almost fell into the fire. The tactics were repeated all over again, Tozer striving all the time to blind his opponent.

They were well matched, but it

seemed as if there was a weakening on the part of the stranger, perhaps accounted for by recent lack of food. He might have gone under but for Beth Adie.

Without any emotion the girl went and picked up the six-shooter that had fallen from Tozer's hand. With equal lack of emotion she walked around the struggling contestants and then smacked downwards with the butt on to Tozer's matted hair.

Tozer was stunned, though he was not altogether unconscious. But it gave the stranger time to get to his feet, where he stood swaying and looking down at his opponent.

Then he looked at Beth Adie with the gun. Beth was staring at him, and there was a curious expression on her face which made him want to ask a question, but there was no time for it at that moment.

Instead, panting, he said: 'I guess I owe you something for that, ma'am. I don't reckon I could've held on to that gorilla for long.'

Beth Adie played with the gun as if she had held one before. She was still watching the stranger. Lightly, almost, she said: 'You shouldn't have walked in on us if you can't take care of yourself. You must have known what kind of men they are, watching back there in the quags.'

She wanted to hear him say that he had come out of hiding to save her, but she was disappointed. Instead, he said: 'I'd got the smell of food in my nostrils. It was more'n I could do to stop out there all night, hungry. I was thinkin' of comin' out of hidin' when this galoot came runnin' after you.'

The girl said softly: 'It was good of you to join in. Thanks, stranger.'

He shrugged. Skulach was groaning and stirring. Tozer had crawled away from the heat of the fire and was on all fours, his head hanging, so that he looked like a sick dog. And a sick dog he was. That had been a hard blow.

Skulach felt for his gun as he came

to. Beth had taken it from him, the stranger realised. That gave her two guns and Skulach and Tozer — none. Skulach stopped being belligerent immediately.

Instead he crouched across the fire from them, his eyes curiously wide now as if expecting no mercy. He wouldn't have given any mercy in like circumstances.

Beth saw that look. She held out a gun to the stranger, saying: 'You don't carry a gun?' The man shook his head. 'Then I guess you'd better hang on to that. If you don't, someone's plannin' to use it on you.'

Old Eb was hanging on to the corner of his hut, swaying weakly. He spoke, but it was in a voice seemingly not addressed to them but as a kind of judgment.

'Them that live by the sword shall perish by the sword. Guns ain't no good to no man. Throw that blamed hardware to the 'gators, stranger!'

Nobody took any heed of him.

Certainly the stranger did not part with his gun. Instead he examined it and smoothed it with hands that didn't look to have been roughened by work in recent weeks. And his eyes were thoughtful as he looked into the distance to where the mist was weaving wraith-like among the low-hanging shadowy marsh trees.

Beth Adie watched him and wondered what he was thinking. Especially she looked at his pants and boots.

When they realised that the stranger didn't seem to have any homicidal instincts, Tozer and Johnny Skulach came edging back to where the fire seemed to promise greater safety than the swampy shadows around them. Old Eb came tottering out on weak legs to range himself beside the stranger and the girl. He didn't say anything. Didn't even look pleased to see the stranger. But clearly he was not in favour of the other pair.

It was an uneasy truce that existed over the quintet. They sat across from each other and Tozer and Skulach in the end even dozed, stretched themselves and went to sleep. But before he slept Skulach asked a few sullen questions.

'You said Slatt's men were just outside. Waiting.'

'So I said.'

'You know Slatt?'

The stranger was fumbling for a few shreds of tobacco. Then he found an old corn pipe and carefully packed it.

That done he answered with a laconic: 'Nope.'

That jerked Skulach's eyes wide open. 'How d'you know that's Reuben Slatt's gang out thar?'

The stranger reached forward and took a glowing ember at the end of a charred stick out of the fire and carefully applied it to his precious pipe. He tossed the stick back into the fire and his eyes lifted to meet those of the blond Johnny Skulach. There was something like humour in the stranger's blue eyes.

'You told me.'

Skulach sat up. 'I — '

'Sure. I heard you talkin' about him to this gal.' His head jerked towards the shadows from whence he had so abruptly stepped. 'Sound travels. I've been lyin' up there for half a day watchin' you — and listenin'. So I know all about this fellar Reuben Slatt.'

The girl looked at him then. 'It was you — ?'

'Sure. I grabbed you.'

'But why?' Beth Adie stared at him, not understanding.

He shrugged. 'You came so quietly up the causeway I never heard you. Almost you trod on me. I jes' looked up, saw you was a gal. I grabbed your ankle to pull you down an' tell you not to go on. I figgered them two skunks was no companions fer a lone gal.'

'But I screamed — '

'Ma'am, you sure can holler! An' you jumped clean out of my grasp afore I knew what you was doin'. It just didn't occur to me I'd scare you like that,' he said apologetically.

'My goodness, you certainly did scare me!'

Skulach looked viciously at Tozer. 'I thought you'd gone to rout him out?' he growled sourly. 'You said he'd done a bunk.'

The stranger said: 'I did a bunk, brother. But I guess I know more ways around this swamp than Bonehead thar.'

Tozer didn't resent the Bonehead. But he seemed less easy because of his younger companion's anger directed against him.

The two men across the fire curled up to sleep. It was the stranger's turn to speak to them.

'You wouldn't be members of Reuben Slatt's gang, would you?'

There was no answer. It told the stranger what he wanted to know. If they weren't members of the Slatt gang, then it was because they had been thrown out of it. That was the explanation for the men's hiding here in the swamp.

Beth lay stretched at the stranger's feet. She felt safe. She also felt wide awake.

'What's your name, mister?'

'Nameless.'

'Come again?'

'I ain't got no name. Leastways, I don't know what my name is.'

She didn't take him seriously and her sullenness returned a little, thinking that he was holding out on her. She didn't speak for a good five minutes, but in the end desire for companionship overcame her momentary anger.

She said: 'What are you hidin' from, mister?'

He sighed and shrugged. Then his head shook slowly. 'Darned if I know,' he said softly. He sucked on his pipe and his eyes stared broodingly into the fire.

'How come you're in this quag?'

He told her part of his story then. 'Around noon today I was snuck up on the edge of the tree belt around the quags. I was watching a farm.

Your farm, I guess.'

'Watchin'? Why?' The girl stared at him.

'I wanted to know what kinda people lived there.' The girl's frown deepened. 'Thar's men in these parts mighty handy with a gun when they see strangers walkin' up.'

The man said it simply enough. But it was true. Since the end of the war and with most of the Confederate forces still in Northern prison camps, this southern land was a prey to wandering no-goods. Everywhere men were on the move, desperate men without any home ties. Men who lived by the quickness of their eye and the slickness with which they threw a gun.

They were like locusts on the land, and that land was already eaten bare by several years of civil war.

'I saw your men ride off this mornin', and I was just figgerin' on walkin' across an' tryin' to get some food, when these two varmints hove in sight.'

The stranger had retreated into the swamps as the pair came up, Skulach being supported by Tozer. Before he knew what had happened they had caused him to go deeper than he had intended into the swamps.

'How did you find the causeway?' the girl shot at him.

The stranger wrinkled his brow and looked puzzled. 'Is that difficult?' he asked, as if there were many causeways and all easy to find.

She shook her head, still watching him. 'There's only one way into the swamps and you happened to find it, stranger.'

Then she looked across at the pair snoozing within the circle of firelight. She was a mighty puzzled girl. 'And they found it, too. Yet they're strangers, I'll swear.'

The stranger said: 'They must have seen old Eb from outside. I guess he wasn't keepin' to cover as I was.'

Eb broke in then. 'I don't ever reckon anyone's interested in these swamps.

That's why I live here. You say they saw me?'

The stranger nodded. 'I'd gone up the causeway to get out of their sight. They were passing. Then you came along the causeway and they saw you and came in. They came up on you when you was drinkin'. A snake bit you then, didn't it?'

The old man remembered. He rubbed his cheek. It was stiff and sore. 'It sure did. Reckon I'm over the wust of that blamed poison now, though.'

The old man dropped out of the conversation at that but Beth wanted to talk. This man was younger than most she met hereabouts, and there was something about him that attracted her. She wanted to make the most of this opportunity.

'Them two.' Her scornful glance indicated Skulach and his companion. 'What brought 'em here?'

Again the stranger shrugged. 'I heard 'em talkin'. Not much. My guess is they got into some row with Reuben Slatt an' they lost their hosses an' had to walk for it in the night. They got here just one jump ahead of Reuben Slatt. Mebbe Slatt was on their trail an' *they* brought the gang down upon your farm.'

Beth compressed her lips at the thought. She wasn't going to like this pair any the more for that.

Then her questions became personal. 'What are you doin' here? You been fightin'?'

'I guess so.' He didn't enlarge upon his words. There was something curious in the way he said them and the girl found she just couldn't leave him alone from her tongue.

But suddenly, unexpectedly, the stranger shot a question at her. He seemed to lean towards her, and there was an intensity about those blue eyes that almost startled her. He was looking straight at her, and then he said: 'You know me?'

She shook her head. 'Should I?'

He persisted. 'Without this beard I'm

carryin'. Would you know me under that, d'you think?'

There was something almost like hunger in his voice as he waited for her answer.

Her eyes studied him in the firelight, and then she shook her head. 'Nope, stranger, I ain't never seen your face before.'

He relaxed at that and seemed to recede from her as if disappointed. She spoke yet again.

'Where did you fight? Which side did you fight on?'

That was an even more important question, here in Texas.

He just said: 'You tell me that.' And when she started to ask questions he said: 'Wait until daylight. Mebbe then what you see will stop you questionin'.'

She was mystified, bewildered, and that stilled her tongue. Here was something deeper than she could understand.

He said: 'We've got guns. But I don't trust them fellars across there. I reckon we've got to keep an eye on 'em all durin' the night. Ef I c'n grab a couple of hours' sleep, I'll be all right tomorrow. Think you can take first trick?'

She nodded. He pulled an old hat over his eyes, rolled on to his side and was asleep in no time. The girl woke him two hours later, and curled up beside a fire that was needed now and went to sleep ignoring the myriad whine of mosquitos and the croaking of bullfrogs all along the marsh. She was safe while this stranger sat guarding her, she knew. She slept well in spite of the discomfort of her situation.

When they stirred with the first grey light of morning, it was to find that the swamps had disappeared. There was a slow-moving mist six to eight feet high that blanketed the world about them, so that only occasionally they saw tree tops floating eerily upon a white drifting sea. Their fire partly drove away the mist so that they lived in a white-clothed world no more than twenty or thirty yards across. The damp made them cold and they shivered.

Johnny Skulach moaned because his wound was stiff. Tozer stirred and helped to sit him up and the two haggard-looking men stared dully around them. They were wet from the night's mist, uncomfortable because they had lain too far away from the fire, and the damp had seeped up through the ground. They were mistrustful of the whiteness about them, too, eyeing it as if expecting any moment to see the gaping jaws of an alligator come rushing at them.

But the sun seemed to bore through that clinging wet mist in a matter of seconds. The moment it appeared over the horizon the mists began to swirl and lift and dissolve, and within half an hour only a few stray wisps were to be seen under the marsh trees. Long before that the stranger and the girl had gone.

When they stood stamping about the dying fire the girl looked at the stranger to find out what was in his mind.

Skulach said: 'We ain't got food. Ain't got no water, come to that. You give us back our guns, mister, an' we'll make our way.'

The stranger was searching hopelessly for more tobacco. He couldn't find it. 'Nope. I've been wantin' guns for the last few weeks. They're hard to come by down South now.'

Tozer looked venomous and Skulach started to bluster. But the stranger ignored them.

He had hoisted Beth Adie to her feet. She seemed to have suffered least of all from the night in the open. But she wasn't happy for all that.

She said to the stranger: 'I don't care where you go. I'm comin' with you.'

His manner and those guns were reassuring. He nodded.

'Guess we'll light out an' find us some grub to eat.'

'Where?'

She was looking at him, remembering what he had said about daylight. The light was growing and she was beginning to see . . .

He shrugged. 'Guess it ain't no good goin' to your place while Reuben Slatt's thar. Mebbe we should light out fer some town nearby an' tell 'em what's goin' on in these parts. Mebbe there's a few men with guts left who'll go out an' help your pa.'

She nodded. If she'd been worrying about her father during the night she had managed to conceal it. Now she said, quickly: 'Say, fellar, what sort of a soldier were you?'

Skulach loked at the stranger quickly at that. His eyes fell on the blue shirt and grey Confederate pants.

Beth said: 'You wear a Yankee shirt and Confederate trousers.' Her eyes fell lower. 'And them's good Yankee boots by the look of 'em.'

He nodded to all that. Beth grew impatient.

'Well, stranger, what's the idea of this mixed get-up? Are you a Yank or a 'Fed?'

She was looking at the stranger when she asked that question and perhaps the moment she uttered it she regretted the impatience in her voice.

Because that short-bearded face opposite her seemed filled with a wistful yearning, a weariness that seemed to say that he had been asked that question many a time — and still didn't know the answer.

His eyes lifted to hers. They were burning. 'I don't know. I guess I'm a soldier. But I don't know which side I fought on. Whether I'm a Yank of a 'Fed, looks like I'll never know. You see, my memory's plumb gone from my head.'

6

They could only stare at him for long seconds on end, not really understanding what he was saying. Almost apologetically he said: 'That's why I'm beefin' around, I guess. I'm lookin' for people who might know my face.'

He turned and walked away a yard or two, and then he wheeled and there was something desperate almost in the way he lifted his hands in appeal to them.

'Don't you see, I must have folks somewhere. Mebbe a mother an' a father. Mebbe, I've got a wife somewhere — even children. Or a sweetheart. An' until they see me they'll think I'm dead.'

His voice became tinged with bitterness.

'I shall be dead, too, so far as they know. Right until they see me or until my memory comes back, they won't know I got through that war alive.'

His eyes flickered from one to the other.

'You don't know me. Looks like I'm comin' through the wrong country. Looks like I'd better drift on an' find another place to start my search.'

His voice was hopeless.

He didn't see Beth Adie open her mouth as if to make a protest at his statement — as if there was something she could say that might help him. And then her lids veiled the betraying eagerness in her eyes and her mouth closed and she turned away. She found old Eb standing there with his faded grey eyes watching her.

She shrugged. Eb was too dull to notice anything . . .

The stranger threw away this mood that oppressed him. The sun's rays were warming through that sheep-herder's coat that partly covered his mixed uniform. He said: 'Reckon I want to get out of these swamp lands afore this mist finally clears. Out there it might come in handy to be able to dodge back in the mist.'

He was remembering the mounted figures he had seen the previous afternoon. As if they were following tracks — maybe the girl's tracks from that farmhouse. Who knows, they might be waiting at the end of the causeway to see who came out . . .

Thinking of that he changed his mind. He emptied one of the guns and threw it some distance away into the bushes. 'I'm leavin' a gun for you. I guess that's better treatment than you'd give me. But don't you move towards it until we're out of sight, get me?'

He looked at Eb then. 'You comin'?'

Eb shook his head vaguely. 'Guess I don't feel up to it. Kinda weak this mornin'. I'll jest' hang around, I guess.'

His eyes looked at Tozer and Skulach and there was the faintest apprehension in them. But he was too weak to walk far and so he had to risk these unpleasant companions of his.

'What about food?' This stranger,

Beth Adie realised, was more considerate than most men she had met. He seemed even concerned for that old man.

Old Eb just turned his head as if the question had no significance. 'Guess I'll live. Guess I've managed times before when I couldn't get good food from people here-abouts.'

His eyes met those of Beth Adie and the stranger in turn and there was the slightest glint of humour in them.

'I reckon to eat most things that can move. They don't hurt me none, but most people turn their noses up at 'em.'

Beth Adie shuddered. She knew there were men like old Eb who lived on anything — snails, hedgehogs, frogs, even beetles. The stranger put his arm under hers and started off along the causeway. He watched the sullen Tozer and Skulach all the while until vegetation put them out of sight. Then he started running, pulling the girl along with him. He seemed to

know his way well. Beth Adie noticed it and did some more thinking.

In fact she was watching this big stranger so much that suddenly she realised she was lost. She pulled back. This path that he seemed to be following led through wilder and more desolate swamplands than she'd seen before. Trees hung close and she was scared because of the snakes they might contain. And at times they walked on strips of land no more than a yard wide, within inches of log-like, almost completely-immersed alligators.

Even the 'gators seemed bigger and more vicious than the ones she knew in her part of the swamps.

She exclaimed, fearfully: 'You've got lost.'

He stopped. 'Lost?' He looked puzzled. 'Nope, I don't think so. I reckon we should come out of the swamp this way.'

He lifted his hand to his head as if to rub away some pain. Then he stared ahead. 'Sure, I don't remember this place but I've got a hunch it's a way out.'

Wonderingly she followed when he walked on. She put her trust in him and an hour later she found it was rewarded.

After a while the swamps grew more solid and the trees looked bigger. Then they found themselves walking through coarse brake where the ground was barely soggy at all. And in time they broke out from this low-lying belt of vegetation and found themselves looking out over a great prairie.

The girl looked at him and shook her head. She was about to say what had been trembling on her lips back in that camp, but again caution came to her and she held her tongue. The stranger was looking round him, a puzzled frown on his face.

He said: 'I can't get over this feelin'. It's funny, but I don't know any place around here, an' yet I've got a feelin' I've been here before.'

His finger pointed over the rolling

mesquite. 'Tell me, Beth, will there be a town over the shoulder of that hill?'

Her eyes were on him. She nodded. 'Yes. A little town. The only one round here.'

His eyes turned and dropped to meet hers. There was wonder in them. He almost whispered: 'Then how did I know it?'

She shook her head. But as she turned away she told herself: 'If he'd lost his memory he couldn't remember such things. He must have been through that town in the last day or so, and mebbe he's just kiddin' me!'

She looked swiftly, resentfully up into his face, but he was looking away now, and the expression of bewilderment upon it seemed all too genuine.

He said: 'We've got a long walk, Beth, I reckon. You gonna try it?'

'My stomach says I've got to,' she smiled, and that was nearly the first time he had seen a smile on her face.

They started off together. She said, after they'd walked a long time: 'I reckon you'd feel more at home on a hoss?'

He slapped his thigh. 'I don't remember ever ridin' a hoss, but I sure would like to come across one and see if I knew how to hang on.'

She looked at his lean, rangy form, and thought: 'He'd hang on, all right.'

She was sure by now that he was a man from these parts, and men from these parts always learned to travel on horseback.

It was two hours later when they came to the little cattle town of Stampede. It was a town of bleached and weathered huts, normally containing no more than five hundred citizens, but since the war with a population less than two hundred.

A railroad ran through the town, but no train had run on it since the early part of the Civil War. The tracks were red with rust and the sleepers rotting and eaten away by insects.

The pair came walking in along the tracks, past the signal on the edge of the town, a signal that would never work again because the winds had snapped off the upper half.

There was no one about the town when they came in, because the heat of the day was upon it, and people didn't parade in the sunshine. They had talked over their tactics on the way in. There was a marshal in the town, a very old man appointed because of his age, while his younger predecessor went off with the Confederate forces.

'I'll go and speak to him and see what chances there are of raising a posse to go and rout out Reuben Slatt and his men,' the girl decided. Then she thought of the four men who had been shot. 'That's murder,' she said, and her hands compressed as she remembered the sight.

The stranger said: 'I ain't goin' in that town. Not 'till I see how friendly the folks are. There's too many people tries to shoot this shirt off me, an' others are lightin' into me who don't like Confederate trousers.'

'I'll get you some new clothes as soon as I can.' There was an eagerness in her voice, a desire to please that was not lost upon the man who called himself Nameless.

He smiled. 'That won't be easy,' he said grimly. 'The South's a land of ragged people. There ain't clothes to be had nohow. D'you think I'd be wearing these darned things ef there were?'

He was looking along the dusty main street, so curiously deserted in that hot sunshine. *She* was looking at him. She was wishing that she had more feminine clothes on than these farm-hand's coveralls. But wishing wasn't going to help her.

She interrupted his thoughts. 'Don't you remember anything?'

He knew what she meant. The frown came back to his forehead. He seemed to be searching back into his memory and finding it puzzling, almost painful.

'Nope. All I remember is jes' walkin'. Walkin' like this. Not knowin' where I was goin' but followin' my feet.

'People kept comin' up an' takin' a dislike to my shirt or pants. They wanted to fight, but I didn't feel like fightin' an' I kept out of their way.

'All I've been doin' ever since is tryin' to find someone who knows me. Mebbe someone will remember me who fought with me on one side or the other. Or mebbe I'll be lucky an' will come across my folks wherever they are.'

She said softly: 'It's mighty important to you to find your people, isn't it?'

His eyes came round to meet hers. She couldn't understand the expression in them, because it seemed again almost to amount to pain.

'You don't know how it is to feel you haven't got anyone in the world,' he said slowly. 'It makes you feel kinda — hungry.'

He shrugged, and it was a gesture to indicate that he couldn't explain what was in his mind, and yet she felt she could understand. But she also felt that she could make use of this big, well-set up man from the wars.

He said: 'I'm gonna sit down in this gully. I c'n watch the town. You tell 'em about your paw, an' see if they'll send a posse out to help him.'

He didn't tell her of his suspicions, that maybe her old man might have suffered since his capture. The girl didn't seem to think of it, either, because she never displayed any great concern over her father's safety. He frowned remembering it. It didn't rate up with his own desire to meet parents and relatives.

She said: 'I'll fix some grub somehow. If it don't seem safe to bring you into town I'll fetch it out to you. But if you see me wave, you'll know it's pretty safe.'

He nodded and she left him. He watched her walk without haste through the dust of the approaches to the town. The road between the buildings had only the most perfunctory of stone surfacing, and it was mostly soil that had blown in from the surrounding desert.

Her form shimmered in the hot air currents that rose in the intervening distance, so that at times she was so distorted that he could barely identify her. But then he saw her climb some steps and go inside one of the single storey, clapboard buildings.

He settled down in the sun, his eyes closed almost, to keep out the bouncing rays that came off the desert soil. He looked half-asleep and yet was completely alert.

He was also watching all around him all the time in the manner of a man seeking familiar places. Yet it all looked strange to him.

Cattle country, and pretty good cattle country at that, he thought. Yet he couldn't recall any features beyond this town. And then the thought occurred to him that through the town along the red rusty rail tracks there would be a water halt. He wondered how he should know that, and yet he felt certain there would be one . . .

Suddenly he saw someone standing in the doorway of that hut into which Beth Adie had disappeared. Distinctly he heard a voice call out and for a moment he thought it was to him. Then he saw figures detach themselves from shadowy doorways where they had been unseen, and come ambling, drooping under the hot sunshine, towards the man in the doorway.

Half a dozen people came, and all were men. Old men, the keen eyes of Nameless told him, watching them.

The men stood outside the office while the man in the doorway talked to them. An occasional sound of voices drifted down to Nameless's ears as he crouched in the gully alongside the rusty railroad.

Then Beth appeared around that little group. She stood in the roadway and put her hands above her head and signalled to him.

That signal had been agreed upon, and yet when it came for some reason Nameless sat in that gulch for seconds without moving. An uneasy thought came to him that here might be treachery. He didn't know why, and yet that thought came upon him at that moment.

Then he growled: 'A gal wouldn't two-time a guy like me!'

He rose, still growling to himself as he knocked the dust off his pants. All the while he was looking round, suspicious of danger — and he didn't know what form that danger might take. He trudged into the town, his manner wary, his hand gripping that Colt inside the pocket of his sheep-herder's coat.

The men outside that office parted as he approached. Beth Adie ran to meet him, and he noticed that she clung to his arm as if possessively. He wasn't quite happy about that action of hers.

She smiled up at him and led him on to the verandah. A man with long moustaches that reached down to his skinny, turkey-red neck was standing in the doorway. A lean old man, a real old-timer.

His eyes looked at that shirt, and then went down to Nameless's pants. He didn't say anything.

But someone in that crowd did. Other people were drifting over now, and most of them were women. A woman, sharp-eyed and sharp-tongued, perhaps a woman suffering a loss of some son in that recent war, shrilled out: 'Take that danged Yankee shirt off, mister. We don't like anythin' like Yankee uniforms around Stampede!'

Nameless turned to look at her, and with good humour said: 'Ma'am, I ain't got no other shirt. You wouldn't want me to go about without a shirt to my back, now would you?'

The men — old-timers all like the marshal behind him — stirred uneasily and spat into the dust, not knowing what to say.

Beth Adie said it for him. 'He's been in the wars, an' he must have got himself hit in the head, because he don't remember anythin' about the fightin'. He don't know which side he fought on, an' he don't even remember how he came by these clothes.'

She looked swiftly at the big young man.

'I reckon he was a 'Fed,' she said with assurance. It brought the tiniest of frowns to Nameless's face, as if he wished he was as sure of that himself.

But her statement made the crowd silent, though they moved restlessly from one foot to another and didn't look upon Nameless with any particular good feelings.

The old marshall spoke. His voice was uncertain because of his great age. 'Son, a dozen ruffians has took the Adie place from Beth's paw. Beth wants a posse to go down an' help him, but I don't reckon we can raise a dozen men in Stampede to match them fellars.'

Beth Adie said, fiercely: 'Not if Nameless goes with you?'

The old marshall shook his head. His

voice was kind but regretful. 'You can see how it is for yourself, Beth. Every able-bodied man got took away into the wars. Right now most of 'em'll be in Yankee prison camps or walkin' across the States to find their way home. We just don't have people to match up to gun slingers.'

Some of the old men talked angrily and fingered guns that weren't much good because they were old like their owners. But all the same, for all the hot talk that came from the old boys, no one really volunteered to ride out to the Adie place.

It seemed all settled in a matter of minutes. There was no helping the unfortunate rancher, Beth's father. She recognised it and seemed to dismiss the thought from her mind.

She smiled up at Nameless. 'I guess we'll find some food in a house I know down the street.'

A girl's voice came from the crowd. 'If it's food you're wanting, Beth, for you and your friend, I'll fix you up.'

Something in the voice made Nameless turn. There were no younger men in that crowd but there were plenty of young women. They wore clothes that were thin with long use, patched and bleached almost colourless by long exposure to the brilliant Texas sun. They didn't look attractive, and most of them felt it and were shy when his eyes moved across to them.

But not this creature. She stood out boldly in that crowd, oblivious to people's glances. He saw a girl who was yet a woman. That kind of girl. The kind of girl who had come out with pioneering stock and made Texas what she was.

A fine-built girl, three inches or so taller than average. Straight as a young fir tree, with a head thrown back on her shoulders that spoke of confidence and pride in herself. She had a good face, too. Good, dark hair that fell in long waves down her back and was gathered by the neck in a faded circle of blue material that served as a ribbon.

She had a bold, intelligent forehead, and eyes that were big and brown and full of the lights of youth — and intelligence, too.

Something in the sight of that girl made Nameless halt. He wanted to look at her and go on looking at her, standing there against that background of other self-conscious, timid young women.

Beth Adie looked up and caught that glance. Fire flashed in her eyes. Nameless found his arm gripped, found himself being pulled along the street, and he sensed the anger in this girl whom he had met in the swamps.

Beth called: 'That's mighty generous of you Jeannie McNay, but I reckon I know where I can get a bite to eat.'

Nameless dragged his gaze away from the girl. Only as his eyes came away did he realise that hers had been locked in his. But other people in that crowd had noticed it, and when Nameless's back was turned they said sly things to Jeannie and made her blush and become curiously uncertain. And that was most unusual for Jeannie McNay.

Nameless felt embarrassed by the way Beth Adie had behaved. There had been too much possessiveness. And yet there wasn't enough in the action for him to protest. It was just mighty good of Beth to find food for him, in a land where food was the most precious thing because there was so little of it.

She took him into a house that was furnished with a plank table and benches, in the crudest of Texas styles. A woman was there, big and raw-boned like a longhorn steer. She was some relative of Beth Adie's and though she didn't seem too pleased to see the girl she at least set food before them on the rude table.

The food wasn't very appetising — a mess of corn mush with a bit of meat in it. It was served grudgingly but was received all the same with pleasure. Both at least were young, with healthy appetites, and even the most unappetising fare was acceptable in their need.

There was nothing to drink except water, but that was good to them after the sour stuff they'd had on the marshes.

Nameless was lowering the jug from his mouth when he heard Beth speaking. There was a quickness about her tone that brought suspicion to him immediately. He could tell when a girl was trying to lead him on, and Beth Adie sure was trying to lead *him!*

'Nameless,' she was whispering, eyes looking back over her shoulder to make sure the old woman wasn't listening. 'Let's get out of Stampede County. There ain't nothin' in Stampede County for either of us.'

He stared at her in astonishment.

'Look, Nameless, I've got a horse.'

'A hoss?' A light came into his eyes. There was a lot a man could do with a horse.

She nodded.

'It's mine. It was sent in to have shoes put on yesterday, and the men were going to bring it back some time today. That was why I was without a horse when Reuben Slatt turned up.'

Nameless sat back on the bench studying that ardent, eager face before him. The enthusiasm of her ideas brought a glow to her face, so that she no longer looked sullen and heavy-featured. In that moment she was infinitely desirable by any man's standard.

And yet as he looked at her he thought of — Jeannie McNay.

Beth's hand was gripping urgently on to the rough material of his shirt. She had got an idea into her head and she was the kind of girl to go all out for what she wanted.

'You don't want to stay here, Nameless,' she urged. 'There's nobody here who knows you or they would've spoken up at that meetin' outside the marshal's office. You'd best ride on, Nameless, if you want ever to meet up with your folk. They ain't in this county.'

'But you can't go with me.'

'Why not?' She had sidled along the form towards him, and now her two hands were gripping his forearm. He felt the warmth of that soft young body close to his, and felt the fan of her breath as she lifted her head to speak to him, her face was so close to his.

Even closer her face came as she whispered, trying with all her maidenly charms to persuade him. She was utterly unscrupulous in that moment.

'I don't want to stay here, Nameless. There's nothin' in Stampede County for a girl.'

Her voice broke bitterly.

'All you do is work all the time at man's work. You go from one chore to another and before you know what's happened your youth's gone.' Her eyes were burning as they looked into his. 'I want to go where there's life, Nameless. To New Orleans, maybe. I want silks and finery, laces and carriages. I want to go to balls and parties. I want to be with young people, and round here there are no young people.'

Nameless looked at her and his suspicions softened. It was true just as the girl said and he could feel sorry for her. This land of Texas was a man's land, and wasn't yet for women. And then he made a mental reservation — it was only all right for brave pioneering women, he thought, and the picture that came into his mind was that of that fine young girl who had spoken out before all that crowd to him.

Because he knew that it had been to him that she had spoken, though she had mentioned Beth's name in that sentence.

He put his hand on hers. 'I'd like to do it,' he said softly. 'But you can't go, Beth. Not with a nameless stranger like me. You don't know me. Besides, there's your paw.'

'My paw can look after himself.' The girl's eyes flashed. There was a sullenness returning to that animated face because of his opposition to her desires. 'I don't reckon he had much love for me, an' I can tell you I ain't got much love for him. He doesn't know I'm around, that father of mine!'

In vexation she turned away quickly and looked out of the window. There was nothing to see but a dusty street and a bleached and sagging wooden building opposite. It was a prospect she wanted to get away from and now her heart was breaking because this nameless soldier was standing in the way of it.

Brokenly she said: 'It wouldn't harm you. I'd be taking all the risks. But we could go away from here. I'd give you that horse. And that's worth a lot of money, ain't it?'

She turned. He was still uncertain. He wanted to go on but he didn't want to tie himself to this girl.

Then there came a blessed relief in their conversation. He lifted his head and listened.

'Thar's plenty hosses around Stampede, after all,' he said, and for a second she didn't understand him.

Then she heard the sound of many

horses riding into town. Her eyes widened. She hadn't heard so many horses since the boys rode off to join the Rebel forces those many years ago. She was at the window in an instant.

Nameless rose, pushing back the bench. He came round the table. Men were galloping down the street past the window, kicking up a great following swirl of dust cloud. The girl could see above the dust, though, and suddenly she was crying out in fear.

Instinctively the nameless man's hand went searching for the Colt, and he jumped to her side and peered out. He saw men on horseback but didn't understand.

Then he saw the United States flag. Even that didn't explain the alarm of the girl by his side.

So he said: 'What is it, Beth? Why are you skeered?'

She turned her face to his. 'You don't need to bother about my paw now,' she said, and afterwards he was amazed that that should be her first thought.

'He's either dead or all right, I guess.' And still she didn't show any emotion.

She pointed after a figure riding alongside the man holding that flag. Simply, she said: 'That's Reuben Slatt with his gang.'

7

'Slatt?' Nameless stared through the window.

He saw the raggedest crew of horsemen he had ever clapped eyes on. They were riff-raff. Men clad in the oldest of rags, some without boots to their feet, so that their bare toes protruded through stirrups that must have been painfully hot to them in that sun. But they were all armed like bandits, and they had their guns out as if intent on using them.

Nameless counted. 'Fifteen,' he said. He turned to Beth Adie. 'I thought you said there was a dozen of 'em at your place?'

'There was.'

Nameless looked after the standard bearer. 'They've got recruits since yesterday, then.'

He grabbed the girl by the wrist, then

shucked on the sheepherder's coat that was too warm in that weather but served to hide most of his Yankee shirt. They plunged out into the sunshine, hugging the buildings but running into the town after the mounted men.

There was a lot of noise. Some of the men ripped off with their guns, in high spirits at the way they had arrived in Stampede town. Reuben Slatt was cracking a stock whip, his red, weathered face grinning jovially at the noise he made. But his eyes were mean as he looked round that town calculatingly.

The marshal came out on to his verandah. Men and women came to their doors. Reuben Slatt brought his horse to a halt in front of the marshal's office, and then he stood on his stirrups and bawled so that all the town could hear him: 'Come on, tumble out, you folks! Guess you'd better hear what we're gonna say to you!'

There was more shooting, a lot of rearing and prancing of nervous horses, and clouds of dust rose up to add to the confusion.

None of the men got down from their horses, not even the thin-faced, drooping-eyed man, so like a vulture, who held that flag.

People came sullenly from their homes, hating that flag that had been a symbol of freedom from oppression for so many.

Nameless and the girl joined in with the crowd, shuffling forward through the dust, trying to look as inconspicuous as possible. The crowd gathered at a distance, as if seeking to avoid the taint of those men who followed the United States flag.

Slatt didn't speak this time. Instead it was that thin-faced, saturnine standard bearer. He handed over the flag to a companion, and then spurred his horse round so that he faced the majority of the townspeople. His back was to the marshal and a few of the marshal's cronies, but he knew he was safe. Reuben Slatt and his men had their guns nakedly out now and were pointing them at the crowd.

A harsh voice rang out, a voice that was thin and nasal and New England in its origin. A cursed Yankee voice.

It was the man who had brought in that flag. He called: 'You folks of Stampede County jest listen to me. I've been appointed marshal of Stampede County, with the full authority of the United States to administer its affairs. If you obey my orders there will be no trouble. But if you want trouble — ' his thin face jutted forward unpleasantly, ' — you'll get it!'

His hand waved to that ragged crew around him.

'This is my posse,' he rapped. 'They too bear the authority of the Government of the United States. They are the law and you will obey them implicitly.'

There was a murmur from the crowd, a murmur that was full of shock at the news. Beth gripped Nameless by the arm. Her voice was scandalised. 'Did you hear? Reuben Slatt and his men, the biggest rascals in these parts, are now officers of the law!' Her scream was scathing.

Some of those townsfolk probably knew Reuben Slatt also, and an angry murmur rose as the news was spread about, so that it sounded like the outraged buzzing of an upturned hornet's nest.

Reuben Slatt, black about the chin for need of a shave, the rest of his face an unpleasant blotchy red, parted lips to show tobacco-brown teeth within. It was a grin that carried no humour. In his face was a challenge, almost a request that someone would give him the chance to use those ready guns of his.

Some of the women were weeping. This was the final indignity. They had given their sons, had suffered years of poverty, and now a band of ruffians had come to take over their affairs. It was not to be abided.

An old man stepped bravely forward. It was the marshal. He said, his old voice high and quavering: 'I ain't givin' in my keys of office to no one. I'm the elected marshal of Stampede County, with the respect an confidence of all the folk hereabouts. Ef you want law and order, I'll knuckle under this hyar flag and administer it. But I don't want to see rascals like Reuben Slatt placed in any authority over us!'

Reuben Slatt turned slowly in his saddle. His eyes trailed deliberately round until they rested upon that old man. It was all so slow up to that moment.

Then like lightning Reuben Slatt struck.

The whip whistled through the air and the lash caught about the neck of the old marshal.

He was dragged to his knees, choking, the blood spurting where the lash had cut into his neck. A scream went up from the women in the crowd.

There was pandemonium. The crowd surged, moving this way and that as crowds do when they do not quite know what course of action to follow.

They wanted to go forward and help that choking old man on the ground, but those guns held by the ragged horsemen were intimidating.

A horse reared and added to the confusion, and then a figure darted under the belly of Slatt's horse and dropped on his knee beside the old marshal. It was the man called Nameless.

Kneeling like that, unfastening that cruel black thong from the flesh of the marshal's neck, Reuben Slatt looked down upon the blue shirt that was so obviously Yankee. His eyes failed to notice the Confederate grey pants below that loose sheepherder's jacket.

He misunderstood the situation and said: 'That's the boy! Mebbe I'll need that lash again on some of these folks. Come on, Yankee boy — come an' join us!'

Slatt looked round the crowd while he was speaking, his eyes almost lost in a merriment that was within himself and apparent to no one else. Silently,

Nameless carefully unwound the thong and threw the lash aside. Then he assisted the old marshal to a seat on one of the worn steps in front of the office. The marshal looked at him without speaking, but there was thanks expressed in his pain-ridden eyes.

Nameless turned round to face the men. Beth Adie was by his side immediately. She had courage, that girl, whatever the unpleasant other side to her character. She was ready to face those hoodlums alongside this bold young man.

Slatt was shouting for silence again, and the other men took up the cry, plunging their horses at threatening knots in the crowd, and hoarsely bawling for silence. Slatt shouted: 'Thar's another lot of announcements you haven't heerd yet. Jes' listen to United States representative Sylvester Quaid.'

A mocking gesture indicated that lean, heavy-lidded man who had brought in the United States flag.

Syl Quaid lifted his hand and when he got silence his voice roared out further edicts. 'Who's the postmaster?'

A man stumbled forward, reluctantly but propelled by hands in the crowd. He didn't want to face the limelight with these desperados in such an ugly mood.

'I am.' His eyes watched that black stockwhip, ready to duck if he saw it coming his way.

Syl Quaid called: 'You *were* the postmaster. But you're a danged Reb, an' you ain't fit to be trusted with the mail. Here, Ned, you take over the post office!'

A grinning, low-browed brute who probably couldn't read an address nodded acceptance of the office from his saddle. A howl of protest went up from the ex-postmaster. Reuben Slatt lashed out with his whip and that sent the man leaping back into the safety of the crowd. Reuben Slatt rolled in his saddle with laughter.

These ruffians meant all they said.

Syl Quaid shouted again: 'Who runs the saloon?'

A belligerent, portly man came striding out from the crowd. His eyes were challenging. 'I do,' he snapped.

Quaid said: 'You ain't got no licence to handle liquor no more. That's a Government licence, to handle liquor, and no danged Reb's gonna get any kind of licence while I'm in charge of this district. I'm app'inting a partner to watch over your affairs.'

That partner was Reuben Slatt himself! To Nameless, standing back with the girl, it was obvious that all this had been pre-arranged before coming into town. And trust Reuben Slatt to take over the saloon with its profitable gaming possibilities!

The saloon keeper snarled: 'I don't need no partner.'

Reuben Slatt slowly coiled that black stockwhip. That done, he hung it neatly over the horn of his saddle. His eyes weren't laughing any more.

With threat trembling on every word,

Slatt said slowly: 'You either take me as partner, brother, or there won't be no need for a partnership deed at all.'

The crowd gasped and flinched and began to draw back. The meaning in the gang leader's voice was all too apparent. The saloon keeper went white. He knew what that meant.

But he was a man of obstinate high courage and he was not going to allow any blackguardly desperado to rule in his establishment. He drew a gun on Slatt.

Slatt must have been sitting with a gun hidden between his saddle and his knee. At the movement from the saloon keeper Slatt merely triggered lead and it passed over his knee right into the heart of that stout old man. The saloon keeper was dead before he pitched on his face.

Reuben Slatt blew away the smoke from his gun barrel. He had killed a man and yet there was not the slightest sign of emotion on his face. Instead a grin appeared, a grin that became bigger and bigger until it seemed to engulf his face. Shocked, the audience heard him call to the new marshal: 'You saw that happen, Syl. He drew on me first. That was self-defence, I reckon.'

Syl Quaid's harsh voice echoed his words. 'It was self-defence. He got what he asked for. And no danged Rebel should be in possession of a gun. He had no right to it and I'll string up any other Rebel I catch carryin' firearms!'

They carried away the saloon keeper, while Syl Quaid made other public appointments. Every store in that town had to receive a partner in order to see there was no 'mismanagement.'

Quaid didn't define the meaning of the word mismanagement, but every one there knew it was a cloak to hide a graft. These desperadoes had come in on the side of the law and were making a racket out of it.

The crowd was sullen. Yet only one person there stood up to the ragged gunmen. That was Jeannie McNay. She had been trying to step forward to say her piece, but friends had held her back, perhaps knowing her outspokenness.

Now she stepped forward as the old saloon keeper's body was carried away. She called: 'That was my uncle you just shot.' It brought the eyes of that mean crew round upon her. Reuben Slott's wicked little eyes flickered appreciatively as they saw that fine, fearless young woman standing out and challenging them.

Syl Quaid called: 'So what?'

The girl's hands clenched and her eyes were bright with an indignation that drowned even the sorrow at the passing of a well-liked relative. 'That was murder,' she said firmly. 'You can call it what you like, but he was provoked and he had cause to draw on you. You all had your guns out and he was aiming to defend his property. It was murder and as long as I live I'll work to get you — ' her finger pointed at Reuben Slatt — 'hanged for it!'

Slatt rolled in his saddle, as if he had

heard the biggest joke of his life. 'She sure is a spitfire,' he shouted, delightedly. 'You'n me could get on fine together, gal!'

The idea brought him straight up in his saddle. He nodded, his eyes looking at her. 'Yeah, that's an idea. Come here!'

The girl didn't move. Slatt gave an almost imperceptible signal with his finger and a man, one of his ragged followers, spurred his horse round behind the girl and cut her off from the crowd.

A sliding movement caused by pressure on the man's knees, and the horse had pushed her within reach of Slatt.

Slatt reached down and grabbed her by the hair. Nameless saw it. It was the second time he had seen a woman so treated in the past twenty-four hours. But it was the kind of thing these men would do, he thought. He started forward, his fist bunching.

Slatt was lifting on that hair, so that

the girl was standing on tiptoes in agony. Slatt was roaring with laughter, as if all this was very humorous. His men were grinning, perhaps, anticipating what was to come.

Slatt reached down with his free hand and ripped at the girl's shirt. It was still ripping when a hand like steel closed over his elbow and jerked him backwards, clean out of the saddle.

Nameless crashed with both knees on to Slatt's body as he hit the hard ground. Slatt was out for the moment, because that fall had been made intentionally hard.

Nameless was kneeling on him, keeping the wind out of Slatt's stomach, a Colt in his hand threatening those other men.

He shouted to the girl: 'Come here, quickly!'

Two girls ran to him, not knowing which one he called to. Beth Adie saw Jeannie McNay running up, holding her torn shirt, and her eyes flashed hatred.

Beth tried to get between Jeannie and

Nameless but Nameless pushed them both aside, growling: 'Don't cover my gun, darn it!'

They were both behind him. He rose from above the gasping gang leader, dragging him on to his knees as he did so. The gun was very close to Slatt's head and there was no need for Nameless to voice his intentions. But he did.

'Slatt gets a bullet through his murderin' head ef any of you galoots so much as lifts a gun towards me!'

He was moving cautiously backwards, trying to get to a corner of the building. Reuben Slatt was recovering and began to walk with him, his hands held stiffly away from his side so that Nameless could see he wasn't going for his guns.

Nameless said: 'I got to have a hoss, you two.' He couldn't stay in that town now, after what he had done to Reuben Slatt.

Beth called: 'Hold 'em a minute! I'll have a hoss for you!'

Nameless stood there, silently covering the mob, while Beth ducked into a livery stable. She was out in a minute with two horses.

Nameless didn't know what she was up to, but there was no time for questions. All around him was a confusion worse than panic. Those citizens of Stampede were bolting as hard as they could go for shelter, expecting gun-talk.

Those ragged desperadoes were shouting with fury, spurring their horses so that they kicked and cavorted about in the dust.

Nameless had got the arm of that ruffian leader wrenched up his back, and he was hurting him so as to make sure Slatt wouldn't get up to any tricks.

Slatt was up on his toes, trying to relieve pressure on that arm and not succeeding. His raw red face was contorted with pain, and he was shouting blasphemies in his rage.

But no one could draw a bead on Nameless. He was partly covered by the thick-set figure of their leader and again the gun was poking out at them.

Jeannie McNay saw those horses racing across towards them and she shouted above the din: 'Get going, stranger! Thanks — and good luck!'

Nameless hurled himself away, Jeannie's words ringing in his ears. It was curious how he should seem to hang on the music in her voice even at such a critical time. Reuben Slatt went flat on his face as the strong arm of the big young stranger shoved him towards those horsemen. Then Beth Adie was right up to them, wheeling the horses round expertly, their manes flying, their eyes rolling the whites wildly, their mouths open as if in excitement at the prospect of a race.

Nameless was alongside them as they came racing up. There was no pause, but with a superb roll the tall man was astride the saddle and racing away.

It was done so expertly that it brought disaster upon them. Beth Adie hadn't expected such skill and her horse got in the way. There was a crash and two horses and two riders came off less than fifty yards away from the Slatt Gang.

8

Nameless hit the dust in a roll. He was on his feet before Slatt and his men realised what had happened. The horses were kicking to their feet, too, and Nameless grabbed one by the bridle.

Beth Adie was rising, not quite understanding what she was doing because she was dazed.

Someone fired. At that there was a general scattering of the horsemen, and then Nameless's Colt leapt into his hand and blasted lead in the direction of those scarecrow horsemen. That made them scatter even more.

It gave him one moment's advantage. He seized it.

The second horse was limping away, hurt. Nameless grabbed Beth Adie round her soft young waist and slung her in front of his saddle. Then he was up and his heels digging in and the pair were away.

They were watching him, in the town, citizens wanting him to escape because of his gallant stand by that girl. And yet they were too wise in the knowledge of horseflesh to expect a doubly laden mount to show its heels to those incensed ruffians. For certain they would catch the pair, those townsfolk thought, and they cursed the ill luck that had brought those two mounts crashing together at such a critical moment.

Slatt saw it all in a flash. Realised that their victims were fleeing but they were at the gang's mercy because in time they could run them down. He jumped for his horse, bellowing orders at the same time.

'Git them pair! I want 'em — alive!' He was snarling in his fury, and they could well understand what would happen to the fleeing pair who had caused their leader's discomfiture. Eagerly they clapped heels to their horses and went jumping down the street in pursuit . . .

They didn't get out of that street, not for minutes. A gun blasted lead across the roadway, and it had the bark of a buffalo gun that had been sawn off.

By the crash of lead into the dry wood opposite they knew this gun was filled with shot.

It brought those horsemen pulling hard back on the heads of their mounts, all anxious not to stop another round from that gun. In that moment of indecision, while the scrub-faced gunmen peered around, a voice called clearly: 'I've got another barrel. Who wants to try it?'

They saw a gun pointing at them from the window of the marshal's office. They couldn't see who was behind it, but no one moved to investigate. That gun in some mysterious way seemed uncannily pointed at every man in that startled bunch.

Someone swore, sitting next to the infuriated Reuben Slatt. 'By gar, that sounded like a woman's voice!'

The horses milled around for a good minute, before Slatt got his senses working again. Then he shouted to his men to spread out, and some to break into the marshal's office from the rear.

He also shouted that whoever was behind that gun would be strung up when he got his hands on him — or her!

But there was no one behind that gun when they got into the marshal's office. Just that gun propped up across the window sill. And it wasn't even a double-barreled gun.

Reuben Slatt and his gunmen had been outsmarted.

When they got into the street Jeannie McNay was standing innocently with some of her relatives outside the hardware store.

The gang didn't even set off in pursuit of Nameless and the girl now. They might have overtaken them, but it seemed as if the heart had been knocked out of them. Anyway, now it would have meant a long gruelling chase through the heat of the day, amid the dryness of a country near to desert in that blazing sunshine.

They went instead to see the new proprietor installed in his saloon.

Nameless wasn't to know what had happened in Stampede town. All he knew was that he had to make as much distance as possible between himself and that township, now under the control of rogues masquerading as United States officials.

In time, though, they both realised there was to be no pursuit, and then gratefully Nameless brought their horse down to a walk. Instinctively he turned its head to follow a track that ran alongside the rusting railroad that traced westward from the town. The girl noticed the action and speculated inwardly upon it.

But she didn't say anything. She was content to sit there against that big man, nestling against his strong young body and feeling the vitality that seemed to flow from him. She was contented, and that was not usual for Beth Adie.

When they were three or four miles from the town, Nameless called a halt. He was perplexed. He looked at the girl sitting before him and said: 'Now, what do we do?'

She shrugged. But that wasn't good enough for Nameless. He shook his head.

'I know what's in your mind, Beth, but it won't do. What about your paw?'

She shrugged disdainfully. 'Him? I tell you he won't even miss me. He ought to have had sons, not a daughter! Now that Slatt has left the old place it settles my mind. I guess my paw is all right now.'

It certainly answered some of the doubts in Nameless's mind, but he wasn't easy in his thoughts. He tried again.

'You can't go with me, all the same, Beth. Don't you realise it? You don't know me. I'm just a fellar without a nickel in his pocket; a man without a name and without even relatives. That's my first job, I guess — to find my folks. I can't look after you an' do that at the same time.'

Her hand was on his shoulder. Her face was turned up to his. She was attractive, and he looked at those soft lips and the white teeth and wondered that he could resist her. She was pleading, whispering.

'I want to go with you wherever you go, Nameless. Don't you see, this country will be the death of me! I've got to get out of it and you can take me with you. I don't ask for anything more than that. Just let me ride along with you!'

Nameless sighed. He was in a dilemma. He could hardly send the girl back, and yet he didn't feel that she should ride with him. He had no particular affection for the girl, for all she was throwing herself at him. And uneasily he thought what people would say about such a situation — especially what Jeannie McNay might think!

Jeannie McNay. It was queer how his heart jumped merely to think of her name . . .

Beth might have been a thought-reader, the way she seemed to understand what was going through his mind. She seemed to compress her lips in momentary anger, and then she redoubled her pleas.

'I tell you, I won't be in your way! And when you get tired of me, I'll leave you without any trouble!'

'But in the back of your mind is the thought that you'll never let me become tired of you,' the young man thought to himself shrewdly, watching that animated face.

She tried her last throw. 'We've got one horse between us. What do we do about it? You need it, and I do. Do we cut it in half and share it?'

Nameless had to laugh at that. For answer he clicked his tongue to the horse and urged it along the trail. Her eyes shone.

'Okay,' he said grudgingly. 'You win,

but not for long. I'll go with you to the next town, and there I'm gonna leave you with your horse. I ain't gonna be sidetracked from this search for my folk. That's the thing that's on my mind, and I ain't gonna let up.'

He was so earnest as he said it that she knew how it must have been hurting him, preying on his mind, this anonymity within himself. Only vaguely, though, could she understand the feelings of this man who had lost everything in life with his memory.

She shrugged at that, well content. When they got to the next town she would try again, she thought cunningly to herself. But at least in getting him to the next town she had got him away from possible competition back in Stampede. She was thinking of that young, spirited girl called Jeannie McNay . . .

They were no more than a hundred yards along their way, just entering a belt of cottonwoods that were as grey with dust as the trail itself. Someone came crashing out of the undergrowth and grabbed for the bridle of their horse. Another grey form was leaping up at them from the bushes. Then another.

The horse reared madly, a man hanging on to its head. Beth nearly fell off the horse, and Nameless was caught by her falling body in the act of pulling out his gun. To save her he had to let go of the gun in his pocket.

Viciously he dug his heels into the horse's side, so that it kicked about and hurled off those grey forms that tried to hold it. Men were cursing.

Nameless suddenly caught the words behind those panting voices — 'Damned Yankee!'

Somehow he got his horse away and came rearing round so that the grey men were all to one side of him. He had Beth held securely across his saddle bow, and his hand was seeking for his revolver.

Panting, the sweat running in rivulets down his dirt-stained face, Nameless surveyed the trio.

They were Confederates.

He looked at their old torn uniforms that had suffered in the field and in the Northern prison camps, too. They hadn't a button between them, and their feet were tied with rags because they were without boots. They were more ragged than the men who rode behind Reuben Slatt, these men who had fought in what they had considered a heroic cause all these years. They were returning poorer than when they had set off. And they were hating this Yankee-shirted horseman as if he were the author of all their misfortunes.

He saw those tired, starved faces of those returning soldiers, saw the savage lights in eyes that had suffered too much, and he could not hate them.

Nameless sighed and slowly his gun dropped back into his sheepherder's coat. He saw the eyes of that dust-grey trio widen at this action. They had been standing in the attitude of men awaiting retribution for an ill-timed attack upon him. They had been sure that death would come to them because they had failed to pull him from his mount.

Nameless knew what was in their minds and shook his head slowly. 'Nope,' he said. 'There ain't nothin' like that gonna happen.'

Then he surprised them even more. Without even looking at them he began to descend from his horse and help the girl to the ground. He swung her lightly off his mount, and she let herself rest in his arms for a second as he gently lowered her.

When that was done Nameless turned to the three men and said: 'You never looked at my pants, did you?' His voice was dry but good-humoured.

Only now did they notice the Confederate grey of his trousers. One of the men spoke, and there was little friendliness in his tone.

'How come you're wearin' a traitor's shirt? I guess a real Confederate would die ruther than wear that danged blue!'

Nameless was watching them and he

didn't attempt to placate them. The girl admired him for it. He spoke the truth.

'I might be a Yankee, for all you know. I might even have been fightin' against you in the past few years. But I don't know. I might be a Southerner!'

'What's all this talk?' The spokesman's tone was roughly angry. 'Doggone it, surely you know which side you fought on!'

Nameless shook his head. 'I wish I did. I just don't know what I've done with my life before a few weeks ago.' His eyes were distant now, as if he was trying to pierce a veil that obscured his memory.

'All I remember is walkin' along a road not more than fifty miles from here. I've got no memory of how I came there or what I've done in my years before.'

He lifted his eyes to that trio and there was that old pain back in them.

'I don't know my name. I don't even know my age. Ever thought what it's like to be a man and not know your age? I don't know where I was born or where I live. I may have parents — a wife.'

They looked quickly at Beth Adie at that.

'I don't know anythin'. All I know is I don't hate any man an' I sure ain't gonna quarrel with Confederate or Yankee provided he's straight with me.'

A young man in the Confederate uniform came forward then. He had hair that was too long but it was curled and gave him a pleasing look. His face was thin and sensitive, and Nameless could see that he was a man of considerable intelligence. Nameless found blue eyes staring at him and there was pity and understanding in them.

'I reckon I'm with you in that, stranger,' the boy said.

He put his hand out. Nameless smiled and shook it. After that there was no need to talk of guns and fighting. They were comrades together, bound together in comradeship by their common misfortune — that they had been reduced to nothing by this war.

Nameless said: 'You look tuckered in. Sorry I ain't got anythin' to give you. We've just had to hit the trail in a hurry from Stampede. I reckon that's where you're goin'?'

The faces of those three returning soldiers shone. 'That's our home town. We've got people in Stampede. It's the end of the trail for us!' It was that intelligent-looking boy who spoke, his eyes dancing with gladness at the thought of the welcome he would get.

It brought a pang to the heart of that bigger man, standing against the horse. He envied them, then, even envied them the rags they wore. Because to them that grey was an honourable uniform, and they could hold their heads proudly, back in their home town. And Stampede was home to them.

Nameless turned quickly away. If only *he* could say: 'This is my home — these are my folks!'

But he couldn't. Not until he found his memory again. His eyes, without him realising it, lifted to look at that railroad. He couldn't understand why he kept looking at it . . .

The men didn't want to stay, so near to their home. They waved, friends now, and started away up the trail. As they walked away that younger man called back. 'I guess you'll be seeing others back along the trail. We passed a few bunches of fellars comin' back. I reckon they weren't as fit as us an' we're mebbe half a day ahead of 'em. But watch yourself, brother!'

Nameless took the girl back to the horse. Silently they mounted. He started to ride away westward, following those twin rusty rails. After a hundred yards he halted the horse and looked back across the shimmering desert between them and the little cattle town. He was frowning.

Beth pushed herself away from his chest. She had been daydreaming. Now her brow furrowed as she caught that backward glance of this big nameless man.

'What's the matter?'

'I'm just thinkin'.'

She became uneasy at once. She saw hard lights in those eyes as a suspicion came to them. She said: 'Thinkin' about what?'

He didn't answer immediately and she tried to be roguish, but her humour was heavy. 'I thought you were thinking about me!'

He ignored her remark completely and that didn't please her. Sometimes his manner made her very angry and she felt she wanted to punish him for it.

He said, suddenly, softly: 'We never warned them fellars what to expect back in their home town.'

'Warned? You mean, about Reuben Slatt and his gang?' He nodded. 'What was there to warn 'em about?'

Uneasily he shook his head. 'I don't rightly know. Mebbe no harm will come to 'em, but I've got a feelin' them grey uniforms might bring trouble on them.'

She tried to urge him on, in her selfishness wanting to get him away from that neck of country. But he was obstinate. And he was uneasy. He remembered that thin-faced, bright-eyed young man who had offered his hand in friendship so easily. He was afraid for him. He was just a boy, for all his uniform, he was thinking.

Impulsively he turned the horse and began to ride across country towards a hill that was covered with camel thorn and mesquite. The sun blazed torridly upon them as their horse gamely picked its way up a rain gully towards the hilltop.

All the while the girl sat stiffly before him, showing in her manner her anger and resentment because he would not go the way she wanted.

But Nameless had only thoughts for those men who were returning so joyfully to their home town. When he reached the hilltop, he swung down, then helped the girl down. And then he ignored her and left her and walked to the side of the slope that gave a view over the bleached and nearly lifeless earth between them and Stampede.

He sat down so that his figure made less of a target against that skyline. That was an instinct born of an experience beyond his memory.

Beth stood behind him, and then, because he didn't move or show any softness towards her, she came and sat beside him, her back again rigid and hostile.

He never even saw her. He was watching three grey-clad figures toiling up a trail that was dreary in its unrelieved monotony. A trail that led into the shanty cattle town of Stampede. His eyes followed them for a full half-hour, and in that time they grew so small their progress was only evidenced by a tiny dust cloud that was lifted by their eager hastening feet.

The dust cloud that obscured the toilers finally disappeared among the buildings that was their home town. Now Nameless sat as rigid as the girl, only he was leaning forward slightly, listening.

Minutes passed. Nameless was on the point of relaxing, when faintly across the intervening space he heard a solitary gunshot. Almost immediately came a second shot.

It galvanised him into action. He was climbing to his feet in an instant, his hand seeking that gun in his coat pocket. The action was automatic, though the gesture was futile.

His straining eyes sought for the town, and then he saw someone break from between the huts and go running into the broken south of the buildings, where the rusty rail tracks looped to cross a rain coulee.

Beth Adie was at his side, watching. They hardly seemed to breathe as they saw other men ride out of the town and go beating about the mesquite. Yet all the while they could see the frantic, scrambling figure of that one grey-clad man, fleeing for safety within a quarter of a mile of the new law officers of Stampede.

They saw the man steadily put distance between himself and the searchers, who must have been thrown on to the wrong track, possibly by the connivance of some stout-hearted citizen of that Texan township.

Suddenly Nameless whirled and went plunging across the hill towards his horse. Beth ran by his side, her face lifted towards him questioningly. 'Where are we going?'

'After that fellar!'

He didn't give her time to debate the idea. He picked her up and slung her unceremoniously on to his horse. Then he swung up and gave it his heels and got it jumping into instant motion.

He rode like a born horseman, the girl noticed yet again. Instinctively he picked land which gave him cover from those men around the town, but all the time he was working his way across country to where the rail tracks ran out into the eastern desert. After ten minutes of quick riding they found themselves on a cutting, overlooking the tracks.

They dismounted and sat against a rock and watched. Unexpectedly their quarry came up off the tracks, stumbling among the rocks in which they were hidden. They heard the tortured labouring of his lungs and the sobbing that went with his breathing. Nameless was on his feet, waiting for the man to stumble into view. He was wondering which grey-clad figure it would be — and hoping it would be that bright-faced boy.

A man came into view. He was staggering in his run, about at the end of his tether.

He saw a horse and a man and a girl standing there, and he came to a halt so abruptly that he nearly fell on his face. He lifted his head and they could see him — could see the torture in his eyes and the torment on his haggard, working face.

It was not the boy. It was that older

man who had greeted Nameless so roughly.

Nameless felt his heart kick in disappointment. He knew what to expect.

It seemed almost as though minutes passed as they stood there watching each other. Then the Confederate moved. He was off his head with grief and he came in to attack the man who wore the hated blue shirt of the Yankees.

But there was litle strength in him after that race for his life, and he came forward stumblingly, almost crawling from step to step. But he came on.

His eyes were wild and raging, and he looked like a man who had suffered so much that Earth had no more torments for him.

As he came in to attack he found breath to shout curses at the big man called Nameless.

'Go on, you damned Yankee, and finish me off! Ef you don't, by glory I'll choke the life out of you!'

Nameless thrust the girl behind him. She was watching the proceedings without any flicker of emotion on her face. Just interested in seeing two men face each other under such circumstances.

Nameless snapped: 'What have you got against me? I haven't done anything agen you. I came here right now to help you.'

'I don't want your help! You should've helped back there. You never said there was Yankees in control of Stampede!'

'Sure.' Nameless nodded. 'It didn't occur to me they'd greet you like they did.'

That Confederate was still lurching forward, his arms swinging, his hands reaching forward to grapple with Nameless's throat.

The Confederate shouted: 'You let us go there. That sticks out a mile. Then you came ridin' round to head me off. You want to hand me back to them damned skunks, your Yankee friends.

But you won't take me alive. I know you've got a gun — '

Nameless spread his hands away from his sides. 'I don't intend to use a gun on you, pardner — '

The man was almost on top of Nameless now. 'I came to try to help you. What happened?'

The man found strength and leapt the last distance. His hands clawed for Nameless's throat. His voice shouted wild curses at this man in the blue Yankee shirt. He was a man beyond reason at that moment, filled with the grief of the loss of good comrades.

Nameless gripped those hands in mid-air and forced them away from his throat. He didn't give ground but braced himself to withstand the assault. His eyes stared grimly into that wild, unshaven face before him. This man, too, wasn't much more than a boy, he was thinking.

'Hold up there. I ain't gonna do you any harm.'

Nameless tried to talk to the man,

but for the moment the Confederate wouldn't listen to him and put all his strength into a savage assault upon Nameless. They grappled and nearly went down, and as they staggered among the rocks the dust was scraped up by their scuffling feet. The voice of the Confederate was silent as he reserved his breath for this deadly struggle.

But Nameless was too powerful for him, and all at once it seemed as though the strength ran out of the soldier. Suddenly he seemed to go limp within the grasp of the bigger man; his knees buckled and he sagged forward, his face drained of blood in a manner that was alarming.

Nameless shouted to the girl to give him a hand. They pulled the ragged-uniformed Confederate into the shadow of some tall rocks and gently laid him down. Then Nameless squatted at his side and fanned him with his hat.

The man slowly began to regain his colour. They heard his whispered voice

— a voice filled with agony — say: 'Why don't you finish me off? I don't want to live now. They were my buddies. We fought together, lived together, now we should die together.'

Nameless spoke almost roughly. 'That's fool talk. You don't want to think of dyin'. Darn it, can't you see there's work to do?'

It shocked both the soldier and Beth Adie to hear that rough tone under such circumstances. Beth's eyes widened. Usually men spoke softly and in a kind manner to the stricken. That is, if they were good men, like this tall stranger seemed to be.

But Nameless knew what he was doing. His words served to shock the manhood back into that Confederate. It even brought a sparkle to the man's eyes, and it was a light of anger that such a tone should be used towards him.

Nameless sat grimly over the fallen man, his lips narrowed, the muscles standing out in the side of his face as if he were clenching his teeth at some thoughts.

Then he spoke again. 'What happened?'

For some reason that Confederate who had wanted to kill the stranger a few minutes before, now found himself docilely answering that question. Nameless had a commanding, authoritative manner about him.

'We walked into the town. We was lookin' for people we knew. We didn't see 'em. There wasn't anybody out in the street at all. That is, there wasn't when we hit the town.'

The man swallowed as if his throat were dry, but they hadn't any water for him. He went on.

'But right opposite the saloon a fellar comes out through the batwings an' takes a look at us.' The Confederate's eyes narrowed, thinking of that moment. 'He was a ragged-lookin' hombre, a hobo an' a no-good if ever I've seen one.

'He'd been drinkin', you could see

that. He was ripe for devilment. When he saw us he gave a shout an' a lot of other scarecrows came tumblin' out of that saloon.

'They walked round us in the middle of the street, an' they said things about this uniform. That didn't hurt us. We've been used to hearin' people say things about us. But what did hurt us was to see a Yankee flag flyin' outside the marshal's office. An' to know that those Yankees — these scum an' hoodlums — were the law and order representatives in our own town.'

Slowly the Confederate hoisted himself into a sitting position. Now anger had pumped blood back into his face and his cheeks were tinged with red.

'I don't know what happened. Them guys was shovin' into us an' makin' sport of us. They'd been drinkin', I tell you. They wanted trouble. They made it.

'I don't know how it started.' He ran his hands through hair that should have been cut months ago. 'Somehow some brawlin' began. We were shoved into each other, an' then someone started to lash out with his fists. The next thing we were all fightin'.

'Ned an' Jim were lashin' out an' they cornered one big thug an' were beatin' hell out of him. He drew a gun. Before anyone knew what was happenin' he'd shot 'em both right where they were. First one. And then, deliberately, he turned on the other.

'He'd have done for me, too,' the soldier said grimly, 'only I staggered agen a door an' it opened agen my weight and I ran through to the back and somehow got away. I figger people in the town were shouting instructions an' pointing all in the wrong direction an' that gave me a chance to save my life.'

He stopped, having said that, as if now it brought back the old problem — what were Nameless's intentions towards him?

Nameless looked at him without smiling and said:

'You're going to suffer no harm at my hands, brother.'

'Brother?'

The Confederate was looking at that mixed uniform. 'Don't tell me you fought on the side of the South?'

Nameless shook his head. 'I don't know which side I fought on, I tell you. Mebbe I didn't even fight at all.' He lifted his hand to his head where a shallow scar showed through his hair. 'Somehow I got hit on the head — mebbe a horse kicked me — but it left me without any memory. Nope. I don't know if I fought for Dixie. All I know is I'm agen thuggery like that back there.'

He jerked his head in the direction of Stampede town. He was thinking hard. Beth Adie came closer, perhaps divining what was in his mind.

She plucked his sleeve and said quickly: 'Now you know what happened to those boys don't you think we'd better be movin'? We've got to ride a long way to get out of Stampede County.'

Her voice was so urgent, so insistent that the Confederate looked at her quickly, then glanced back towards the big blue-shirted man and regarded him covertly under half-closed lids.

Nameless was looking along that rusting track. His brow was furrowed. He wiped the sweat from his dusty face before speaking. He was having to make a decision, a decision he didn't like, but some inner force compelled him towards making it.

Then he said: 'I don't reckon I'm goin' to ride out of Stampede County, after all.'

She tried all she knew to win him to her side. She had decided to get out of this country and she was selfish enough to play upon any emotion to get her way. He saw those bright eyes that were near to anger and then she was saying: 'But what about your people?'

'They'll still be there, wherever that is, in a few more weeks' time, I reckon. Right now I figger there's a much more important job around here.'

'Job?'

He nodded. His voice was hard. 'Sure. It goes agen my grain to see scum masqueradin' as victorious soldiers an' holdin' a town to ransom because they made a deal with someone carryin' the Stars an' Stripes. Nope, I reckon I'm gonna stay here an' help dig 'em loose from their hold on Stampede.'

Beth jumped away, furious. 'But you can't! What can one man do?'

'Two men.' Nameless's gesture included the Confederate. The soldier was standing now, life back in his eyes, waiting eagerly to hear what this big confident stranger had to propose.

Nameless wheeled on the girl. 'You can quit talkin' about runnin' away,' he thundered. 'Goldarn it, you ought to be ashamed of yourself, talkin' of runnin' out on people who need us!'

The indignation in his voice was so genuine, it stung. Beth Adie retreated a step, as if the force of his words had physical weight.

'Don't you see,' Nameless said, 'there'll be others comin' back along that trail — '

'I told you we passed quite a few of the boys limpin' home.' That was the soldier's eager voice.

'We've got to watch out an' warn 'em not to go in to meet the trouble that awaits 'em in Stampede. An' we've got to do more than that.'

They were waiting on his words, both faces turned intently towards him. The girl's sullen, not wanting to hear what he said. The Confederate's, gaunt and unshaven, eager, alive and suddenly alert.

Nameless shifted uncertainly from one foot to the other, as if struggling to formulate his thoughts. He was still sweating, and his eyes were staring into the distance — the distance beyond the little cowtown of Stampede.

Slowly he spoke his thoughts: 'We've got to fight back agen them low-down scum!'

9

'Fight?'

The Confederate was standing there now, his hands clenching and unclenching. That word put the heart back into him.

'Yeah, fight.' The face of that nameless wanderer was ridged with tight muscle as he clenched his jaw when he had spoken. It was a fighting face, a fine face, they both suddenly realised.

Get that beard away from him, the girl was thinking, and here would be a man any woman could be proud of. Anger flared into her at the thought. An anger that came of frustration. For she had been near to the point of getting this man for herself, only they had come upon the unfortunate Confederates just at the wrong moment. Now she knew she had lost him, though she told herself it was only for the moment.

In her heart was a determination to work upon him and by hook or by crook to get him!

Nameless was still thinking, his eyes withdrawn from his companions, standing there in the shadow of the big rock on that sun-drenched boulder-strewn slope.

'They're gonna do harm to Stampede an' the people of Stampede. You can see what's in their mind. They're ridin' under the protection of that flag, an' they intend to soak the people of Stampede for all they've got. An' with it all there'll be bloodshed — fights an' killin's. An' them poor people in Stampede — old men an' women an' children — they won't be able to fight back.

'So *we've* got to fight for 'em, savvy? We've got to raise our own forces to strike at them an' cut 'em down.'

'Where are you goin' to get your forces?' The girl's voice was ironic.

Nameless pushed out a brown, strong

finger until it touched the grey uniform of the soldier.

'Here's where we'll get our rough riders,' his voice suddenly rasped. 'Them 'Feds, straggling back to their homes, will be just the fellars to take up the gun agen Reuben Slatt an' his damned gang!'

He wheeled on the Confederate.

'What's your name?'

The man answered simply: 'It's Joe. Joe Cullen.'

'Mine's Nameless.' Joe Cullen's eyes widened. But Nameless didn't have time to explain. 'Joe, we're gonna sit across that trail from now on, an' we're gonna see that no other unsuspectin' 'Feds walk into Reuben Slatt's arms. We'll take it in turns to hide out on that trail.'

'An' when we meet up with 'em?' Joe Cullen was ready to follow this big man anywhere now, with this inspiration he was giving him. Fight back, the big man had said. Joe's teeth gritted together at the thought, and his eyes burned.

He would give his life to fight back against these murderers of his comrades, he was thinking. And he was also thinking that this nameless man was the right man to lead them against the Border ruffians.

'As they come up the trail, Joe, we'll take 'em to a hide-out of ours.'

'Hide-out?' Beth Adie wouldn't keep out of the conversation. 'Where can you find a place to hide an outlaw gang?'

'Outlaw?' That was Joe Cullen, surprised.

The girl almost jeered. 'If you fight against that flag you'll be outlaws, won't you?' She was angry and in an unpleasant mood, wanting to hurt.

'But Slatt's men are scum, they're not really law representatives,' Joe Cullen protested.

'She's right,' Nameless said gently. 'That's somethin' we'll have to point out to the boys when we meet 'em. They're scum, them Slatt's men, but they've got that rascally United States marshal to make them peace officers.

So, whatever we say, to take arms agen 'em means we take arms against the new United States law. That makes us — outlaws!'

Joe Cullen gritted his teeth. 'Then by God, I'll be an outlaw,' he swore.

Nameless nodded approvingly. They were his sentiments. Here was something wrong, and regardless of the cost to himself he was going to fight against it.

'That hide-out,' he said thoughtfully. He was looking along the track that ran through this cutting into the hills. It was rough ground, pretty good for men in hiding. But not good enough, he knew. Men had to have shelter from the sun and the winds, and the night's cold in these parts.

He was also thinking that the men coming in would be weak and weary and it would be days before they were in shape to follow him. And there'd be need for horses . . .

He said: 'I've got a feelin' that right over them hills should be a shanty town.' His hand lifted to his head, as if trying to press out the reluctant thoughts that came from a stilled memory.

'I don't know how I remember, but I'll swear thar's a shanty town right over that cutting. An' my memory says it's deserted. Ef that's so, we could hide out in comfort until we're ready to strike agen the Slatt mob.'

Beth Adie was standing back from him, as if the better to see him. Her bright eyes were regarding him with a curious mixture of thoughtfulness and dawning understanding.

She said, abruptly: 'How do you know there was a shanty town back there?' He didn't notice she said 'was,' and it was on her lips to say: 'You have lived in these parts before, though no one knows you — lived here for quite some time or you wouldn't know as much about this country as you do.'

But she didn't say it, because she didn't want him to stay in this country. She wanted to be away from it herself, and she was selfish enough to want to use him as a tool to get away from this desolate, uninteresting territory that she had known too long.

Nameless didn't answer. His mind was racing towards more practical things. Food and horses. He lifted his head, remembering something.

'That shanty town's right on the edge of the mesquite that runs up to your ranch, Beth.'

She nodded, sullenly waiting upon his next words.

'Beth, thar's a job for you, a mighty important job. Men need food. You'll be able to get food for them.'

'Who says I should?' Her voice rose with anger near to breaking point. 'We haven't food for more than ourselves, back on the farm!'

Nameless ignored her temper. He had a purpose in mind and he was the kind of man not to be swerved from that purpose under any circumstances.

'You can go into the town to help out with food.' He smacked his hands together. 'That's it. You c'n go where we couldn't show our faces. You'll be able to get word to the men's relatives an' they'll give you food to feed 'em. An' mebbe we'll fix up ways of findin' horses. We'll need 'em agen the Slatt mob.'

In his mind he was already building up his plans. This would have to be like a military operation, with his men living off the land. They would need spies in the enemy midst, and those townspeople would be ripe for the job. There wouldn't be an action of Slatt and his men which wouldn't be seen by watchful eyes, and everything could be reported back, to be made use of.

He began to think that if those unfortunate people knew of a growing force building up outside the town, they could be incited to furtive acts of sabotage to help the cause.

There were so many ways of harassing an enemy and reducing their confidence. Something thrown on to the roof of their sleeping quarters in the middle of every night, for instance. Men who lose sleep lose their nerve, he was thinking. And the blacksmith could shoe their horses with bad nails so that they were forever kicking off. His mind raced round to the many possibilities.

'They're a mighty tough bunch,' he said grimly. 'And we've got nothin' — we're short of men an' hosses an' guns. But by glory, we'll have Reuben Slatt glad to ride on an' leave Stampede as a bad memory in his mind!'

He turned quickly to Joe. 'We're gonna move, brother — fast! Come on, let's find our hide-out!'

Beth said, suddenly: 'Hold on.'

They halted irresolutely. She was trying her best to upset the big man's plans.

'There's one thing you've forgotten. Which side did you fight on, Nameless?'

He shrugged, puzzled. 'What's that got to do with . . . this?'

'A lot. You're takin' arms agen the United States flag. You're goin'' to become an outlaw, you've said that yourself. But you might be doin' somethin' even worse — you might be . . . a traitor!'

'A traitor?' That shocked him.

'Yes. Suppose your memory comes back. Or suppose some of your old comrades somewhere recognises you and prove that you have been a Yankee and not on the Southern side in the Civil War. They'll point the finger at you and say you are a traitor leading your old enemies against their side. And they'll be right. You won't be able to stand against that charge. Because you'll be leading men all wearing the uniform of the Confederate army.'

There was triumph in her voice, shrill, unpleasant triumph. She felt she had placed an argument against Nameless's plan, an argument that could not be overlooked.

'You can't take the risk. You'll have all the forces of the United States army agen you! Once they know someone's leadin' Confederate rough riders they'll be after you an' they'll hound you down and you won't get any mercy. They'll shoot you like a dog! Their tempers are still running high after the Civil War, don't forget. You're a fool if you take the risk!'

There was despair once again on Joe Cullen's haggard face. His eyes turned to look at the big man called Nameless. There was no hope in those eyes now.

Even Nameless seemed to flinch at the thought. No man likes to feel he is a traitor.

Uncertainly he said: 'Mebbe I wouldn't be a traitor.' His eyes lifted quickly. 'Who's to say I am a Yankee? Mebbe I'm a Reb, too. Then,' he shrugged, 'I'd be just another outlaw, and no one would take much heed of me. Only traitors get the attention. We'd clean up this town and mebbe no one would ever know about us or bother about us, as just a pack of Confederates out to make their home town safe agen ruffians.'

'Fine talk,' she jeered. Then the hard

false smile left her lips and her face was set and contemptuous. 'I'm sayin' you're no Reb, Nameless! You've got a lot about you that seems Yankee. I think I know who you are!'

She turned away quickly, having said that, as if regretting her statement immediately the words had left her lips. A quick light came into the big man's eyes. Almost he leapt forward to take her by the elbow.

'You know . . . me?'

'Mebbe.' She was sullen again.

'Tell me,' he insisted. 'What d'you mean?'

'They have told me something,' she said enigmatically. She was pointing to the twin rusty ribbons of steel track below them. She wouldn't explain any further.

Baffled, Nameless withdrew. He realised that the girl had some clue to his identity, though obviously she did not know him personally. Still, even that clue would have been something to follow up, if only she would speak.

She tried to use it as a bargaining counter.

'Forget these crazy ideas, Nameless. These people in Stampede don't mean anything to you.' She was desperately pleading with him now, completely selfish in her desires. 'They're not your folk. If you've got folks at all, they're not here. But you come away from Stampede County — ride off with me — an' I'll tell you how to begin to find out something about yourself.'

It was a temptation. All this man's burning, concentrated thoughts of these last three weeks had been to find some clue to his identity. It was ironic that when the first hint should be given him there was this other demanding thought in his mind.

Joe Cullen saw the struggle in his mind and didn't attempt to help him. He stood there between them, waiting, without any hope in his heart. What this girl had said in these last few minutes — that word 'traitor' and this promise to help him find out about himself

— seemed arguments against helping strangers at the risk of his own disgrace and life.

But unexpectedly that fighting brown face went hard and purposeful. His eyes almost disappeared into grim slits as he looked at that girl.

'Beth Adie, I wouldn't make a bargain with you at that price. Doggone it, gal, you ought to be ashamed of yourself, thinking only of yourself and not those other people!'

Hope flooded back into that wasted Confederate's body, hearing those words. The light of almost happiness leapt into his eyes as he looked at that big man, so angry suddenly with this girl who had tempted him.

'Beth, it would be a rotten thing to do, to run out on these folks right now. I don't care if I was a Yankee! I don't care if I am plannin' to lead my old enemies agen the flag you say I might have served. I don't care for any of that.

'All I know is that good, decent folk — aye, Rebels, mebbe — are bein' harassed and held to ransom by scum like the Reuben Slatt gang. Scum not fit to live in the same world as decent men and women!

'Sure, there'll be people who say I am a traitor. Sure they won't stop to ask questions — they'll call me renegade, an' they'll go to any extent to hound me down and shoot me out of hand.

'I know all that. An' I know the risks I'm takin'. Here's one good thing I can do even if it's the last in my life. And here's somethin' you can do that's pretty good, too, Beth. What's more, gal, you're gonna do it!'

She almost shrank from the intensity of his words. He had grabbed her by both arms and was almost shaking her in the fierceness of his emotions. She was jerked right out of her mood of sullenness. Almost she was scared of him in that raging, burning mood.

She saw that brown, well-muscled face staring down at her and she listened to his next words, almost not understanding them.

'Beth, you're gonna help me — you're gonna help these people of Stampede, rather. They need you an' you can't let them down. Once they've been helped, then mebbe I'll be able to help you an' you'll be able to help me. That mightn't be long from now. What's another four or five weeks in your life out here, anyway?

'You're goin' to be our eyes in that town. You're goin' to be the link between our hidden force an' them folk back in Stampede. You're goin' to be our go-between, carryin' messages an' orders an' instructions — orders an' instructions that'll make Reuben Slatt wish he'd never ridden into Stampede behind any gol-darned United States marshal. An' you're going to feed us — you're goin' to find the food an' bring it out to us, savvy?'

And Beth Adie — sullen Beth Adie who had never done anything for anyone except grudingly in her life before — found herself nodding, agreeing to this forceful man's demands. More, she was so shaken by the virility of the speaker that there was no intention in her mind of even going against his plans afterwards.

Joe Cullen watched in amazement, astonished to see the effect this vibrant, commanding big man had upon that selfish, obstinate girl. Suddenly he stepped forward, his hand outstretched. Both men gripped.

Joe Cullen said: 'You may be a damned Yankee. But if it's ever proved, I'll still say I'm proud to have met you.'

Nameless's tight face slowly relaxed. It was as if the emotion was draining out of him. Quietly, tiredly, it seemed, he said: 'Thanks, Joe. That was mighty nice of you to say that.'

He turned. There was a lot to do. He wanted to make that shanty town quickly, so that then he could ride back to watch the trail and prevent other Confederates from walking upon their enemies. Beth Adie watched him pityingly as he began to lead his horse over the rocky hills. She knew of the disappointment that was ahead for him.

They walked quickly over that rough ground beyond the end of the cutting. Out on the other side they had a fine view of the rolling mesquite, and in the far distance they were able to see the farm that was part of the Adie ranch. They could also see the steaming, low-lying belt of vegetation that marked the swamplands.

But there was no sign of any hutted camp on that plain. Nameless stared as if trying to make a shanty town appear before his eyes, but there just wasn't another building in sight save for the distant Adie ranch.

He muttered: 'I must have been wrong. Of course I was wrong. Yet I could have sworn . . . '

They walked their horse down to the edge of the track where it ran into the mesquite. Then Nameless halted, his hand pointing, a dawning light in his eyes.

'I was right,' he almost shouted. 'Look!'

He was pointing to marks in the

grass. Grass which grew in patches of a different shade to the surrounding, more flourishing mesquite. And there was rubble about, some of it in significant straight lines. As if earth and stones had been dug away to make foundations for . . . buildings.

'There was a shanty town here. I was right.' He turned fiercely upon the girl. 'I've been here before. I don't know people around these parts, but I know this country. That shows I've been here. Why didn't you tell me they'd moved this shanty town?'

Joe Cullen said gently: 'I could have told you that, too. I was here when this shanty town was built. It sat here for about nine months while the railroad engineers dug a way through this hill.'

His head jerked to indicate the cutting through which they had ridden.

'But when they were through they struck camp and loaded everything on to freight cars and got them through to build another camp west of the hills.'

'But I've been here! I was in this camp!'

Nameless's eyes flickered to meet the girl's. 'That's your clue, isn't it? You realised that in some way I was connected with the building of this railroad.'

It explained a lot. His knowledge of this country without being known to the local inhabitants. His memory of places that had once existed like this hutted camp.

Beth Adie turned away, suddenly feeling sick. Sick because nothing was going right, and because of that mounting frustration that seemed forever with her and seemingly could never be dissipated. Now this big man knew as much about himself as she did. She felt that her hold upon him, her power to control him in the future, was slipping, too.

She walked behind them as they explored that camp, and her thoughts were bitter and burning. She vowed to herself that she would still bend this man to her will. Now she wanted this man more than she wanted to leave this country. And when Beth Adie wanted anything she was utterly unscrupulous in the way she got it.

Finally, Nameless had made up his mind. 'We're goin' to your place, Beth. Your paw will be glad to see you safe, I reckon, anyway.'

Beth's thoughts were: 'You don't know my paw!' But she said nothing.

Nameless continued: 'Joe needs rest. Ef that gang's left your ranch, it'll be safe for us to hide out there. We'll bring the other Rebs in to rest up there.'

'And if Reuben Slatt's men think to ride back for anything?' Again that sullenness.

'We'll have men watchin''. At the first sign of danger we'll take 'em into another hide-out, one that Reuben Slatt won't know of.'

He was thinking of the swamps. He, Nameless, seemed to know them better than anyone, and certainly none of Reuben Slatt's men would know their way into that alligator- and snake-infested quarter. It would be a good hiding place in an emergency.

It took them the better part of two hours to reach the Adie ranch. Most of the way Joe Cullen had to ride, because he was weak from his exhausting experiences, and lack of food told on him. Sometimes Beth Adie sat behind him, but she was independent and refused to stay long on the horse and preferred to walk silently by the side of the big man called Nameless.

He trudged as if tireless across that sun-baked mesquite. Rarely did he speak. Now he was planning.

He knew all too well how desperate were the days ahead of them and he knew it would be folly not to think carefully now and plan cautiously well in advance.

When they were near to the Adie place, standing back against a wind-break of trees that had not fallen to the woodman's axe, Nameless walked with greater caution. But he knew they must have been seen, walking across that open expanse of prairie, so they continued without slackening their pace right up to the high mud wall before the ranch house that was a relic of Spanish days.

The place seemed deserted. It had a forlorn look about it, as if even in a few hours it had gone to the dogs.

There were four neat graves on the outside of that compound wall, and they did not need to be told whose graves they were.

Inside the compound Joe Cullen dismounted while Nameless and the girl went cautiously up the front steps on to the verandah . . .

Nameless suddenly clutched at the girl and halted her. Some sound had come to his ears. There was someone moving among the trees behind the building.

Whispering quickly, he said: 'Stay there!'

Then he went sidling round the corner, his back to the bleached and warped boards of that frame building that had taken the place of the more graceful, habitable Spanish *hacienda*. His gun was ready in his hand. Joe Cullen came up behind him to help.

Nameless went cautiously round to the back, where rusting farm equipment obstructed the way. A man was standing under the trees, sullenly facing them, as if he had heard their approach.

Nameless went forward boldly when he saw he had been seen, but though that gun hung by his side it was ready for instant use.

He saw a heavy man, a man of faintly familiar and unpleasant features. An oldish man.

The man's eyes flickered from one to the other and he seemed surprised to see them. He came forward a couple of steps hesitantly. Then he said suspiciously: 'What do you want?'

Nameless put his gun away at that. He said: 'Your name Adie?' The man nodded.

Nameless shouted: 'Beth, I guess

here's your paw!' Beth came running round the corner.

Nameless watched the greeting between the pair. There wasn't much demonstration of affection. The old man looked a bit relieved, and that was all there was to it. Beth never even said she was glad to see her father. Clearly these two had grown apart from each other in the years they had lived in this desolate place.

The old man said: 'I was back here fixin' some things to take with me. I reckon I wasn't lookin' out, pretty sure them varmints wouldn't come back yet awhile. So I didn't hear you until you were right inside the compound.'

'You thought we were probably Slatt's men returning?' That was Beth speaking.

Her father's face contorted with rage. 'Don't breathe that name in this place ever again!'

When Nameless looked at him he saw marks on the man's face, as if he had taken more than one beating. By the light in those eyes he had suffered at the hands of the Slatt gang and was filled with hatred towards them.

Nameless asked politely: 'You were goin' some place?'

'I *am* goin',' corrected the old man grimly. He went back under the trees and brought out a pack and a blanket roll. This he slung on his shoulder. 'Yeah, I'm goin' out of this county. I'm goin' to find some law officer who'll be strong enough to stand agen Reuben Slatt an' his Yankee friends.'

Nameless watched him steadily. 'You'll have a long walk, old-timer. There won't be any law officer in Texas who'll dare go a-gunnin' agen Reuben Slatt while he's got that flag to protect him.'

The old man said: 'I'm still goin'. I ain't gonna stay in this doggone country any more. I've got no men now. I reckon I've lost my stock — it'll be wanderin' in the hills, an' I've no one to round 'em up. I might just as well get out of this country while I've got two legs to carry me.'

He looked fiercely at his daughter. 'My mind's made up. D'you want to come with me, daughter?'

The girl hesitated. Her glance stole up towards Nameless's face. The old man was watching and he didn't need to be told what was in that look. Perhaps in that moment he recognised what he had failed to realise before, that his daughter was a woman and had her needs and desires like any other woman.

Beth didn't answer him. The old man just turned and began to walk away. Nameless went after him with a couple of long strides. His hand grasped the old man's shoulder. Adie turned to look at him.

'You don't need to go, old-timer,' Nameless said, and there was sympathy in his tone. 'I'll have men in this place within a day or two. I'll run this ranch for you in return for our keep. What d'you say about it?'

The weary, discouraged rancher took

time to answer that question. Perhaps he had been bitter before because there had seemed no hope, and with no hope there was no sense in staying in this land. But there was a way about Nameless that inspired his listeners. It inspired the old man now. Suddenly it seemed to him that perhaps all was not over, that perhaps the right thing was to stay on and fight it out, whatever there was to be fought.

Long minutes seemed to pass and then the old man sighed and let the blanket roll drop from his shoulder.

He grunted. His eyes looked around that crude but familiar home of his — the home that had been his for so many years. All at once he knew he didn't want to leave it, and with the assistance of this big, resolute stranger, maybe there was a future in Texas after all.

He started back to the house, and Nameless picked up his bundle and followed him . . .

Dawn came with a swirl of mist

floating in from the distant swamp-lands. Nameless was up early, saddling that horse. Beth came round to the stable.

She said: 'We're right out of food, except for some dried meat. You're welcome to that for breakfast.'

He nodded. He knew there was little food in the ranch-house since the departure of the Slatt gang. He said: 'I'm hopin' you'll have guests today. I reckon you ought to go into town an' fix up some food. Whisper the word among some of the people.'

He nearly said: 'Like Jeannie McNay.' And then he realised how unfortunate that remark would have been.

'Try an' fix yourself with a buggy and a horse. There'll be people willin' to give you everythin' to lick them skunks with their Stars an' Stripes flag. Don't be scared to ask 'em for what you want, Beth!'

He said he would come back for the girl and give her a lift almost into the town. But she would have to walk into

Stampede after that, because he would need this horse himself.

Her brow furrowed. 'You don't aim to set off for that trail right away?'

He shook his head. He was looking towards the swamps. 'We might need that place. If Slatt's men tumble to what we're doin' on your spread, they'll come a-gunnin' an' then we'll want to take refuge in the swamps.

'But maybe you've forgotten who's in that place right now. Skulach an' Bully Tozer,' he said grimly. 'Two mean, pisenous hombres, if ever I've met any! I've got to dig 'em out of that swamp so that if we have to go in there in a hurry there's no one holdin' us up, *sabe?*'

She nodded. He swung into the saddle and went off without eating. That could wait for his return from the swamps.

But when he rode his nervous, skittish horse along that causeway between the stinking swamps, he found only Eb in possession. Skulach and Tozer had gone within an hour of

Nameless's departure the previous morning, old Eb told him.

'I reckon they were skeered that if they didn't go you might tip off the Slatt gang where they were.' The old man spat ruminatively into the mud. 'I reckon they did something mighty bad agen Reuben Slatt. Now they sure tremble when they think of that galoot and the revenge he'd like to take on 'em.'

Nameless studied the old man's face. It was swollen where the snake had bitten him a day or so before, but there were other marks on that face — bruises such as he had seen on the face of old man Adie.

'Them skunks beat you up?'

Old Eb nodded as if it was unimportant. 'A bit. Just out of meanness. They couldn't forgive you for beatin' 'em an' walkin' off with their guns.'

Nameless nodded. He said, his tone frosty: 'I'll beat 'em up for you if ever I see them varmints!'

He rode back to the ranch after that, leaving old Eb with the promise of food if he visited the Adie place later in the day. Old Eb seemed indifferent. He was nearly as much a creature of these swamps as the lizards and snakes and beetles that lived in it.

Nameless grabed a quick bite and then swung Beth before him on the saddle. She liked it. She put her arm under his and held him tighter than she need have done. He knew it but said nothing.

He had work to do, bitter dangerous work, and Beth Adie wasn't going to interfere with it. If Beth liked rubbing close against him, he thought with grim humour, that didn't hurt *him!*

He dropped her outside the town, where low rolling hills gave cover from watchful eyes among those dreary, huddling buildings. He saw Beth well on her way up the dusty track that wound over the hill, and then he set his horse to ride by circuitous route to the trail that came in from the west.

An hour later he found a position in some drooping cottonwoods and there he dismounted, eased the cinches of his horse and lay down and waited.

He spent most of the next week there, and in that time eight weary Confederates came up that trail and were intercepted. They were suspicious at first, but in the end walked with him to the Adie house. Because of their suspicion, in fact, as soon as some of them were fit enough to ride the horse, Nameless let them lie in wait for their comrades.

At the end of a fortnight they had twelve men in Confederate grey uniforms hidden out at that Adie ranch. They had also the beginnings of a considerable espionage service within the town of Stampede.

But they received news which dashed their hopes of ever outnumbering the Slatt gang.

Beth drove in on a buggy that had been lent her by citizens in on the secret. She had food in boxes under the seat and this was quickly removed by Confederates inside the compound. But Nameless saw trouble on the girl's face and he went and asked her point-blank: 'What's worryin' you, Beth?'

She sighed. 'You'll never do it, Nameless. The best thing's for you to forget all about this idea and move right out of the county.'

He shook his head. 'What is it?'

She said: 'Slatt is calling in all the gunmen along the border to share in the spoils of Stampede. In the last two days men have been riding in all the time to join Slatt, and they're saying in Stampede that he's got over thirty followers as blackguardly as himself!'

10

The town, quite truly, was being held to ransom. Now every business had its 'partner.' And those partners were taking most of the money or valuable produce. By Beth Adie's account the town was now a licentious place, with women of their kind being imported to make the saloons the more acceptable to the prosperous rogues.

'Stampede people are sending their girls out of harm's way into the hills,' Beth Adie said. And then she told of the fights that were flaring up, of the old men who were being assaulted when they tried to protect their womenfolk.

Nameless listened and all that he heard determined him on his course of action. They could no longer wait to build up a superior force. Now they had to strike!

He said so to his followers and they

looked at him in amazement. Joe Cullen voiced their feelings. 'Strike? How can we strike, Nameless? There's a dozen of us — thirteen includin' you — and now we're told there's more than twice that number of Slatt's men in Stampede!'

Then he added the most significant remark of all.

'Sure, we've all got guns by now — of sorts. But we haven't got hosses an' this ain't no country for fightin' 'cept with good hossflesh between your knees.'

Nameless argued stolidly: 'We can't sit still any longer. Tonight we're goin' to raid Stampede. Tonight we're goin' to get all the hossflesh we need out of Stampede. They won't be expectin' us and we shall be able to get away with some of their hosses. But you know what it means when we do get away with their cayuses?'

One of the boys in Confederate uniform said, quickly: 'War!'

'War!'

Nameless nodded. 'They'll be after

us from that moment, knowin' there's a band of men in the neighbourhood and that band can only be aimin' agen them. So, from tonight the war's on!'

They knew they were outnumbered. They knew that in any fighting the terms would be unequal. And yet those men, sick of the news they had been hearing and tired of hiding away in this ranch-house on the sun-drenched mesquite, raised a cheer.

It did Nameless good to hear that support. It was hazardous and he was glad there were no doubters among his followers.

Beth Adie shook the reins and drove off behind the house and the way she went showed her feelings. She hated these Confederates now because they appeared to stand in her way. Without them, she was thinking, she could have got out of this hell-hole of a country, with Nameless to look after her until she found a more attractive place to spend her life.

Old man Adie alone watched her go,

and alone among that audience he guessed the temper of his daughter and divined something of what was in her mind.

He was not a sensitive man and he was to be blamed for the way his daughter had turned out. Yet nevertheless there were times when he remembered that he was her father and then he regretted her sullen, bad-tempered behaviour. Now he realised that his daughter was not with them in this enterprise — that she only remained with them out of attraction for this big, commanding-voiced nameless wanderer.

Nameless lost no time making his plans. They had three horses, including the two in the buggy.

'Reckon that means most of you will have to walk into Stampede.' He looked at them. Nobody was bothered about that long walk after dark.

'Reckon we've done plenty walkin' in the past few years an' a few miles more won't hurt us none.'

There was a growl of agreement at Joe Cullen's words.

'You'll be ridin' back, anyway,' Nameless said. 'I'll go ahead right after sundown. I want to get word round among your people to keep indoors at all costs when the fightin' starts. We can't have women and old men wondering what it's all about and comin' out to see.

'You'll all come quietly into the town an' meet me back of the freight offices.' There were plenty of buildings back behind the freight line's depot, with deep shadows that would cover their movements, and it was far enough away from the saloons to guarantee that the Slatt gunmen would not be around.

Then, he told them, they would sneak out and get away with the Slatt mob's horses hitched to the saloon rails. 'If we do it quietly we can be right out of town before they know what's happened.'

'I thought you said we were gonna have a fight?' That was was a redhead speaking. He looked mean at the prospect of going to Stampede without having a crack at the Slatt men.

Someone growled at that: 'Aw, let's git them hosses afore we starts thinkin' of gunplay, McNay.'

McNay. Nameless brought his eyes round quickly to look at that tall red-haired young Rebel. Before he could control his tongue he found himself asking: 'You Jeannie McNay's brother?'

The boy nodded. When Nameless looked up there was Beth Adie standing on the verandah looking down at him and listening. She turned away and went into the house and the way she flounced betrayed her anger. Nameless felt a stab of misgiving, seeing her. He didn't trust Beth Adie much at all.

Later that afternoon, when they were all trying not to think of the hazardous expedition that night, Joe Cullen routed out his leader. He found Nameless in the bunk-house with the other men, taking it easy during the heat of the day, knowing there would be little sleep for them that night.

Joe said: 'I've still got a fellar lyin' up in the cotton-woods waitin' for other Rebs to come along. Nobody's been up that road for four days now. We reckon not many other fellars is likely to come along now. D'you want us to keep a man there? Won't we need him tonight?'

Nameless hadn't thought of that. He said: 'Better bring him in, Joe. Take a hoss an' give him a lift back.'

Joe Cullen didn't turn away immediately. There was something else on his mind, and he seemed mightly pleased with it. He grinned unexpectedly at the big fellow, lying comfortably in his narrow bunk.

'Come on, Joe, let's know what's pleasin' you!'

Joe wrinkled his nose and said enigmatically: 'Thar's plenty white flour bags back in the store-shed.'

Nameless cocked an eye at him. 'Come again?'

Joe said: 'You know what you said about gettin' on them fellars' nerves? I've got an idea! I reckon we ought to wear masks, but I reckon we could do the job a bit better than just wearin' handkerchiefs across our noses.'

Nameless rolled on to his side. He and Joe Cullen were fast becoming buddies and he respected Cullen's advice and ideas. So now he waited, confident that this would be a good suggestion.

'I reckon we ought to slit them bags, makin' long strips of 'em. We could use 'em as bandages, bandaging the whole of our heads.'

Joe got a bit excited at his own idea, because he had a picture in his mind.

'Don't you see, Nameless, we'd be masked but we'd be masked in a way no one's ever seen before. We wouldn't be just ordinary outlaws, we'd be *bandaged men!* We wouldn't look pretty, either. We'd really scare the life out of them fellars when they saw us!'

Nameless swung his long legs over

the edge of his bunk. Some of the other men were listening, interested. The big fellow said: 'Joe, you've got yourself one hell of a grand idea there!'

His eyes sparkled. This would terrify some of the Slatt mob. Mebbe not tough Reuben Slatt himself, but the more cowardly ones. He could just picture his dozen rough-riders, silently riding into Stampede on some occasion, with the moonlight showing up their bandaged heads. It would be enough to terrify anyone.

He made up his mind. Gave an order. The bags were brought out at once, washed and dried within the hour in that hot sunshine, and then carefully cut into long bandage-like strips.

When Nameless rode off after dark he was carrying a roll of bandage in his pocket. The men who were coming on foot started off with him, but he knew he would gain a good half-hour on them, riding into the town.

He went straight to the house of Jeannie McNay. He knew where it was because he had taken young red-headed on one side and questioned him about his home.

He rode carefully into the town, noting that the moon was just beginning to rise when he walked his horse into the shadows behind the freight station. Dismounting and tethering his mount to a door handle he crept quietly along the street to where the McNay house stood. Jeannie McNay lived with her parents over a trading store almost at the end of the main street. He found the house without difficulty, and facing the street with its lighted saloon and gaming establishment windows, he furtively tapped on the door.

Someone crept quietly to the other side and he heard a whisper: 'Who's that?'

Nameless answered, equally softly: 'Your brother's friend. Let me in.'

There was a hesitation, and then the door opened slightly. He saw a bright eye looking up at him, trying to distinguish his features in the near-darkness. He tried to help her. 'Mebbe you remember me — I came in with Beth Adie, the other day.'

The door was opened in an instant.

Nameless slipped into the dark passageway and immediately the door closed behind him. They were in a darkness that was absolute. Nameless suddenly felt his heart thumping as he sensed the presence of this lovely young girl so close to him in the blackness. He felt the warmth of her soft young body as she brushed against him. Then her hand caught his arm and he found himself being led into a back room. The shutters were up against its windows, but she did not attempt to light the lamp.

Perhaps she guessed his surprise for she explained: 'We none of us ever light our lamps now at night. Slatt's men think it good fun to take pot shots at lighted windows. So now we don't light lamps. We sit up in darkness when night comes — or just go to bed.'

Nameless had a sudden impression of a town under siege. Of a wearied, fearful people sitting night after night behind locked doors, not daring even to light their lamps. They would be sitting all around him in the darkness right then, he thought, praying for the moment when their fighting young men would liberate them from these drunken rogues who were bleeding the town dry.

His jaw clenched in the darkness. The fighting young men were going to strike back that night! Within a few hours the townsfolk would know that the fight was on, that Slatt's men had had their day. For Nameless was determined that whatever the odds against them this was one fight they were going to win. Right would prevail. Right *must* prevail!

Jeannie pushed him down into a crude wooden chair. By the creaking sound when she sat down he guessed she was sitting on the edge of her bed. He wished that he could see that lovely, fearless face and cursed the darkness that hid her from him.

She said: 'My parents are in bed. And — and there's someone else in the next room, so keep your voice down.'

Nameless wondered at that, but he spoke softly in obedience to her desire.

'We're out tonight for the first time,' he told her. He heard the quick intake of her breath. 'Yeah, we've waited long enough. Now we're beginning to fight agen Slatt's mob.'

He told her of their plans.

'We need hosses before we really start to go for Slatt's mob. So tonight we aim to steal their hossflesh right from underneath their noses. I guess that's the only way we can get hosses.

'You, Jeannie, must go round from house to house warnin' your people what to expect. We don't want any one on our side to get hurt. So tell 'em to stay indoors at all costs. When the fun starts tell 'em to keep low so they don't stop any stray bullets.'

Even as he spoke he wondered if he was doing right in asking Jeannie McNay to undertake this important job. For this meant that Jeannie, alone of her people, would be out in the streets that dark night, and his heart missed a beat at the thought of her perhaps running into some of Slatt's men.

Even while those thoughts were occurring to him there was a sudden outbreak of revelry from one of the saloons close at hand. Clearly the gunmen were beginning their night's enjoyment down at the saloons, and in that mood they would be ripe for any outrageous conduct.

Jeannie must have known what was going through his thoughts, for she said: 'You don't need to worry. I'll get word to every house in the town within the next hour. And no Slatt's man will ever see me do it, you can depend on that.'

Again his heart warmed towards her, because of this resoluteness that was such a part of her character. He found himself thinking of Beth Adie and comparing the two.

He stiffened in his chair. There had been a creaking sound close to his head. He sat like that for seconds in the darkness and then relaxed, thinking it would be just the warping of this crude wooden building.

Jeannie said: 'What time do you expect your men in?'

He said: 'They'll be along within the hour. But I can hold 'em back until I know you've been round the town. I reckon no one's goin' to walk into the freight yards at this time of night.'

He began to tell of the disguise they would adopt to add terror to their raid — and he was fumbling in his pocket for the bandage to show the girl what was in their minds. Then he realised she couldn't see it in the darkness. He wasn't thinking very clearly, he chided himself, and he knew why it was. This girl's presence seemed to make him heady, as if he had been drinking. This certainly was a wonderful girl . . .

The door right against him was

kicked open. A light fell blindingly upon them — and yet it was only the light from an unshaded candle.

Nameless crashed his chair, tilted Western fashion against the wall, on to all four legs. He dived to where Jeannie's form was suddenly revealed across the tiny room from him, sitting on the edge of her bed. He was instinctively seeking to protect her, by intervening his form between her and this potential danger. His gun was coming out.

Jeannie grabbed his arm and held the gun within his coat pocket. He turned.

Bully Tozer was holding that candle. Johnny Skulach had a gun pointing straight at his heart.

Nameless gasped. 'What — '

Skulach and Bully Tozer seemed just as astonished to see him. For a second they all stood looking at each other. Then Skulach's quick voice exclaimed: 'What are you two talkin' about?' His eyes danced quickly, suspiciously, from Jeannie's face to Nameless's. 'We heard you talkin'. You ain't plannin' treachery?'

Jeannie pushed Nameless on one side. Again she was forthright in her actions and words.

'You can put that gun away, Johnny Skulach. And you can stop using words like treachery where I'm concerned.'

Her eyes blazed indignantly.

'When you came to me I told you you'd be safe in our house. You are safe. I won't hand you over to Reuben Slatt, so get those ideas out of your head!'

Skulach relaxed a little, but his mean eyes glared at Nameless. 'He wears a Yankee shirt,' he said nastily.

'He's agen Reuben Slatt, that's all you need to know,' the girl snapped.

She strode forward indignantly and pushed Skulach's gun down. It was a brave thing to do and Nameless held his breath, for Skulach was meaner than the water-moccasin that had bitten a hole in old Eb's cheek. Yet such was the strength of character of this girl that she did it and got away with it.

Nameless let out his breath in a great sigh. He relaxed his hold on his gun and showed his empty hands to the pair. 'We don't want gunplay between us,' he said acidly. 'I don't like you or your pard, but my fight's agen Reuben Slatt and his scum.'

Tozer just watched him silently, waiting for his cue from Skulach. Skulach hesitated, remembering the way he had been defeated by this tall man of mixed uniform. His mean soul cried for revenge at any price.

But that mean, cowardly soul also craved safety for his own skin, and he knew that if he started firing it would only bring the Slatt mob to his hide-out.

He shrugged. His hand came away from his gun.

Tozer looked at Skulach as if in surprise, as if he couldn't believe that Skulach was going to let his enemy escape. But then Tozer couldn't see more than a few minutes ahead of him.

They made no move to leave that

doorway until Jeannie said sharply: 'You're not wanted here. I'm talking to my friend. Go back to your room — I told you you're safe enough. And put that candle out. We've got shutters but always some light escapes and you know what happens when the Slatt mob sees a target for their guns.'

Her vigour drove the two men out of the room. She closed the door just as they blew out the candle. Once again Nameless was in the darkness with her.

Suddenly she was standing right against him, and her hands were gripping his arm just above the elbow.

He heard her whispering, and her face was so close that he felt the warmth of her breath upon his cheek. It took all the self-will and determination in him not to put his arms around her. There was that craving upon him again, the craving that had come to him a few times since he had seen Jeannie McNay out on that sunlit main street less than two weeks earlier.

He heard her say: 'I don't like those men!'

He whispered back: 'What are they doing here?'

'They were skulking back of the houses, desperate for food and water. When I heard they were on the run from Reuben Slatt I had to give them sanctuary. They're hiding out with us until Skulach's wounded shoulder is better. He couldn't last long, walking the mesquite with a shot-wound like that.'

Nameless thought: 'Sure, gal, I understand. You're too big-hearted to turn your back on a sick dawg.' And Skulach was a dog all right.

Aloud he whispered: 'They're pisen, them two. They were part of the Slatt mob not long ago and you know what kind of men follow Reuben Slatt. You'll get into trouble over this, Jeannie.'

She said, simply: 'What can I do? I can't turn them out in their condition, and I can't hand them over to Reuben Slatt.'

He knew she was right. He said: 'I only hope they didn't hear what we were saying earlier.' He wished he hadn't sat so close against that door. It was surprising how even whispered words travelled far in the night's stillness.

Then he said: 'Let's go!'

For he felt that he couldn't stay in this darkened room with this girl any longer and not take her in his arms and kiss her. He had work to do, that night, anyway, he told himself resolutely.

Jeannie had work to do also. She took his hand and led him back down the passage and quietly opened the door so that once again they stood out on the main street.

She said: 'This is where we say goodbye. But do come again some night to see me, won't you?'

It was naive, that direct invitation. It told him what he wanted to know, that she was attracted by him, too. He liked her for her directness.

'I'll come if it's safe,' he promised,

and there was more than a promise to it — it amounted to a vow, and she knew it.

She squeezed his hand and silently glided away. He stayed in the shadows where he was, watching her, his hand on his gun in his pocket, ready to protect her if any reveller tried to molest her.

He heard her tap at a door, heard her whispered words, and then her shadow flitted on to the next house. He saw her right down the street, and then she started along the opposite side. She was working back now towards the saloons. He would not leave her until he had at least seen her past this danger point where the saloons and gaming establishments were centred.

He hated it, standing there and letting that girl risk her safety going from house to house. There was a pandemonium of sound rising from all the bars now. The liquor was circulating freely among these rogues with their new-found wealth. They were spending their money fast — lining their cunning leader's pockets at the same time — and judging by the sound, they were in a mood for any boisterous mischief.

Nameless heard the high-pitched laughter of the women who had been brought as hostesses in the various establishments. That kind of woman didn't help in a time like this, he thought. Those ruffians wouldn't be able to distinguish between those trollops and a straight girl like Jeannie.

The moon was up, casting long shadows and bright patches about the street. A few men occasionally staggered out from the saloons, mostly going from one bar or gaming place to another. When this happened Jeannie froze in the shadows, and big Nameless's gun came out to cover that potential danger.

But every time the reveller staggered harmlessly into some other lighted establishment and then Jeannie continued on her way.

Nameless moved at last when the girl

waved to him to indicate that the main street had been warned. Now there were the houses in the back alleys — still not safe for her, but now he could no longer watch over her, as he had done along the main street.

She was on her own.

Nameless sneaked away through the deep shadows, finding a route to the freight yards. It took him some time, because he was uncertain about his bearings.

When he got there, however, he found the place deserted save for his horse. It was taking his men longer to get into the town than he had anticipated.

'Reckon they're sneaking in mighty cautiously,' he thought, and he approved of the caution. Men on foot would be helpless and at the mercy of these mobsters if Slatt received warning. That was why it was so important to get horses that night, so as to equalise terms.

In spite of himself, however, there

came a time when he was definitely uneasy. He kept looking up at that rising crescent moon, and thinking that the men were later than they should have been. Little stabbing fears came to torture him. Perhaps they had been detected and held up! Perhaps after all they had lost their nerve and abandoned the project! Perhaps . . .

But there were a thousand things he could think of at that moment to explain the non-appearance of his followers.

And then, suddenly, there was the faintest of movements behind him, right where the brilliant white moonlight bathed the churned-up dirt before the freight line's wagon sheds. The movement was of something just edging into that moonlight, something stealing out of the shadows towards him.

Nameless lunged for his gun and came moving swiftly sideways into the deepest shadow he could see. That Colt lifted to cover the intruder. His finger tightened on the trigger and his jaw was set. He would shoot if his safety was threatened!

He saw it. Something for the moment that chilled the very marrow of his bones. An awful, unearthly figure seemed to build up in that moonlight just beyond the velvety black shadow.

It was a grey ghost of a man with a hideous bandaged head.

In spite of himself Nameless felt the hair on his head stand upright and gooseflesh shivered in waves down his spine. He had expected his men to appear like this, but even so the ghastly appearance was as much as he could stand.

He relaxed, a mighty sigh of relief exploding from his tight-drawn lips. He was thinking: 'My glory, but them Slatt's men are sure gonna get a shock when they see my pretties!'

All his 'pretties' were stealing into the yard now. They came over to him. He said in a whisper, drily: 'Brothers, I don't like the looks of you!' He could hardly believe that under this fearsome disguise were the friendly faces of the comrades he had made in the past few days.

But their voices were familiar. Joe Cullen's, especially. They gathered together in the shadows, whispering. While he was giving instructions Nameless was rolling his bandages around his head. That done and the end tucked in, he knew he was ready for their night's desperate work.

It was less uncomfortable behind that bandage than he had expected. He had wrapped it so that his mouth was free and his nostrils uncovered. And there was a slit so that his vision was unimpaired. That was going to be important, later.

Those men stood silently before him, listening. He told them what had happened, that Jeannie was still going the rounds, warning their people. They must be careful, then, not to open up at the first movement — it might be Jeannie!

Then he called Joe Cullen. 'Joe, our plan won't quite work out. Not more than three or four hosses is hitched to that rack. The rest, I guess, are in the livery stable. That means they've got to be saddled up and that's gonna take time.'

He told Cullen to take half the men and hold up the owner of the livery stable and saddle all the horses they needed.

'The rest come with me. We're gonna take up positions down the main street so as to cover Joe and his party. If there's shootin', we'll fall back on the livery stable an' ride out on whatever hosses are ready.'

It was the only thing they could do. They split up, accordingly, and the men dissolved away into the distant shadows. Nameless silently led his own men down the main street, flitting from shadow to shadow and not moving when anyone turned out of the saloons. Once they had a scare as two drunkards staggered almost straight across to them, and then entered an alley without noticing the crouching figures in the deepest shadows.

Nameless clung to the board sidewalk, edging his way to a position opposite the principal saloon in the town, within which would be the bulk of Reuben Slatt's hucksters. In this position he knew they would be able to hold back any number of men for a few vital minutes if warning got through in some way to Slatt.

They stood there in the shadows of doorways, spread out down the street. It was only after a while that Nameless realised that quite inadvertently he was standing in a familiar doorway. This was Jeannie McNay's home. He hadn't seen her since that final wave at the end of the street. She might be indoors already, and he hoped so but he felt she must still be making the rounds of the townspeople.

To check up on the house, to make sure this was Jeannie McNay's, he edged his way along the sidewalk. It was the McNay place, all right, he thought grimly, and then his eyes behind those tight-pressing bandages caught a movement between the darkened shutters.

At once he stepped back into the shadows, listening. His heart was pounding, and the hand that gripped his gun was white at the knuckles as a suspicion leapt into his mind.

'Skulach and Tozer!' was his immediate thought. That pair of evil men would be inside that room. They must have seen him; must have guessed who he was if they had overheard his earlier conversation, in spite of that hideously bandaged head.

But what could they do to hurt him? he reassured himself. Their interests were almost identical to his own. They could not betray him to Slatt, he was thinking, without betraying themselves to their own enemy.

And then Jeannie McNay came into the main street.

Ill luck was with her. Horrified, Nameless saw her struggling in the grip of those two drunken gunmen who had staggered a few minutes before down that darkened alley. They must have stumbled right on to the girl as she called upon a householder!

Nameless saw every detail of that scene down the main street. The moonlight was brilliant, bathing the three approaching figures in a white light that was almost dazzling.

Jeannie was struggling silently between two men who were enjoying themselves. Silently . . . Nameless realised why, even in the midst of her terror, that girl was holding her tongue. It was to give the Bandaged Men their chance.

The men, out in the main street, weren't so silent, however. They were beginning to curse the girl for her struggles. But in some sort of good temper, for all that. As if they liked a girl with spirit and didn't mind a struggle — provided the struggle didn't go on too long.

One of them suddenly began to

shout, calling to companions within the main saloon. He wanted witnesses to their sport. Nameless heard his drunken voice loudly slurring: 'Come an' see what we got! Ain't she just the little hell cat! None of your tame, board women for us. We've got a local gal, an' by Jiminy, ain't she just got spunk!'

Someone came through the batwings. Someone else was right behind.

Nameless knew at once what was going to happen. Their plan had miscarried. Another few seconds and the horses would have been ready for them, he calculated, and they could have gone for the two roisterers and then made their escape. In anguish he thought: 'Oh, god, just for another half-minute or so!'

For that reason, because the safety of his men and ultimately the safety of this entire town depended upon their need for horses right now, he held back from going to help this girl who meant so much to him. Jeannie would have to suffer at the hands of these men for a little while longer in order to help their cause, and he knew she wouldn't mind doing it.

It took tremendous self-control to keep Nameless from plunging to the rescue of this girl, nevertheless. He stood in the shadows, his gun pointing towards the nearest of those two drunkards, and the men beside him heard him growling curses under his breath.

Away down the street Nameless could hear movement in the livery stable. Horses were stamping, as they always did when they had been saddled and were eager and ready for the trail. They had to gain a precious minute or so, he thought, and then they wouldn't be so helpless.

But if they were seen before they were on horseback, he knew they would never get out of this town alive. There were too many of their enemies, and they wouldn't get far on foot with men able to scour the district on horseback.

Curiously, little was happening outside that saloon before them. It was as if the drunkenness of the men concerned slowed down their wits. A tiny hope began to creep into Nameless's breast. Nothing much was happening to Jeannie, except that more men were standing by those batwings, roaring approval as she fought in the grip of her two captors. If this could keep up a little longer they might yet save the situation . . .

Right at the moment when hope flared in his mind, because he could see horses coming out of the lighted livery stable along the street, there was treachery.

Almost in his ear someone's voice rang out with startling clarity: 'Watch out, there!'

It was Skulach's voice.

Skulach was a man who never forgot an injury. Probably at this moment he reckoned he could down an enemy and escape detection himself. So, deliberately, he called attention to those seven lurking bandaged men on the opposite side from the saloon.

At the cry every eye came swivelling round, probing into the gloom. The sharpness of that warning was sufficient to drive away the mists of alcohol from their brains. They were born to a life of danger and the warning sent their hands instinctively to their guns. Even the two men holding Jeannie swung round, clawing for Colts on their thighs.

They were seen!

A voice roared: 'Look, there's fellars watchin' us — '

Before that sentence could be completed everyone across at the saloon had seen the crouching men. Nameless shouted: 'Git Jeannie clear!' And he jumped forward, diving towards the pair who had been manhandling the girl.

Those bandages probably saved their lives. It had been an inspiration of Joe Cullen's, after all. For the sudden appearance of those hideously-bandaged heads in the bright moonlight was sufficient to send those gunmen jumping back in astonishment. They didn't even pull trigger for those vital few seconds that gave Nameless his chance.

He wanted to save ammunition. He would need all the bullets in that revolver in a moment. So he came in with his left fist driving.

He saw Jeannie McNay's face, bathed in that moonlight, looking towards him over a captor's shoulder. He shouted: 'I'm comin', Jeannie!' And instantly there was a glad smile on the girl's face, recognising his voice. Her trust was complete in him . . .

Nameless saw a bewhiskered face. Saw a sagging jaw that betokened the horror in the man's mind at sight of this bandaged apparition that was leaping towards him.

Nameless shut that mouth with a vicious left hook that sent the man sprawling into the dust.

Then Nameless was tearing into the other man, lashing into his stomach. In a whirlwind couple of seconds Nameless had hammered the man away from Jeannie. The other Bandaged Men were crowding round the girl now, protecting her.

It was a Bandaged Man who let go with the first round, and Nameless had a hunch it was Jeannie McNay's red-headed brother who started the shooting.

Instantly every gun in those Bandaged Men's hands leapt to life, and lead spewed towards those bewildered, astonished gunmen outside the saloon.

The volley sent the men diving indoors for safety and that gave the Bandaged Men their chance to flee.

Joe Cullen used his head. There was no time to bring up horses, so he turned them all loose and lashed them into a gallop down the moonlit main street. They heard him shouting: 'Git aboard! They're all yours, fellars!'

Nameless twisted his bandaged head and saw a stream of horses plunging down the narrow street towards them.

He hurled himself backwards out of the way, dragging Jeannie with him. His men didn't need to be told what to do. As gunmen within the saloon opened fire over the window sills and around the edges of the doors, man after man swung himself at full gallop into the saddles and went streaking for the safety of the darkness and the mesquite. Joe Cullen was bringing up the rear with his mounted followers.

Jeannie shouted: 'I'm gettin' indoors! Look to yourself, big fellar!'

She was gone in an instant. That absolved Nameless from any further responsibility. As the last of these horses came racing through with Cullen and his men, big Nameless took a sprawling dive at a coarse black mane. His fingers clutched. His body turned in a practised roll that got him on to a bare back. He'd picked an unsaddled horse!

It had no bridle, either. But it kept running after the other horses and that was all that mattered.

There was frenzied shooting from

Reuben Slatt's baffled gunmen when they saw these daring riders get away with their horses. Two of Cullen's men stopped lead, but neither was wounded badly enough to knock him out of the race.

They rode in a wide circle, going westwards so as to throw the Slatt gang off their track. When they came to the rocky country beyond the rail track, where hoof-prints would not show, they began a circling movement of the town, continuing until they finally made the mesquite with the long straight gallop home.

It had been a good night's work. They had only just made it, though, big Nameless thought grimly. Still, now he had men, guns and horses! Now they would truly be able to fight back against these gunmen masquerading as peace officers!

But as he stretched himself wearily on his bunk later that night, the glow of satisfaction that was within him arose from another thought.

He knew that Jeannie McNay was his for the asking.

The thought carried such a thrill that he could think of nothing else that night. No longer did it seem so important to be on his way to find his family and know his identity. That could wait. No one would be hurt by a lapse of a few weeks in his memory, he consoled himself. Jeannie McNay was the important thing in his life now.

And he never even gave a thought to Beth Adie, lying sullen-faced, awake in her bed in the ranch-house. If he had known of her thoughts at that moment he might not have been so happy.

11

By their action in stealing the horses that night, war was declared.

Until that moment the Slatt gang hadn't suspected enemies in the district — at least, formidable, armed enemies. But now they knew it. It must have been obvious to them at that moment that their reign of terror over the town was threatened.

Nameless knew they wouldn't quit Stampede in a hurry. This life was too good for them, with no work to do and plenty of money to be had for the taking, and more fun at nights in the saloon than they'd ever known before. Yes, he thought grimly to himself, it was pretty good to be running a town in the guise of peace officers.

He called a meeting of his Confederates next morning. 'We've got to work fast now,' he explained. 'They're rattled because they never expected what happened last night. But Slatt is a bold man and he'll attack back as soon as he's got chance. So we won't give him any rest.'

Nameless led the war on the gang himself. It was a war on their nerves, they all realised. For the Rebel force was outnumbered, outgunned, and that didn't promise victory for them for the future. But resourceful men could make up for deficiencies, they all realised.

Nameless went thundering down the main street of Stampede in the middle of the afternoon, shooting his gun in the air to announce his dramatic arrival. He was wearing the bandages around his head, and he knew he must look a fiercesome object.

Right opposite the main saloon, his left hand jerked a parcel through the doorway of that surprised institution. Then he was away, racing along the westward trail before the Slatt mob could do more than fire a few rounds after him.

When they opened that parcel Slatt's men found a note inside. It read: 'Reuben Slatt. Take your men out of this town or we'll hang the lot of you. You are not peace officers and we are not standing for your presence in Stampede any longer. You have been warned.'

It was signed: 'The Bandaged Men.'

It was disturbing. Slatt cursed luridly when he received that bill and promptly went to his friend, that thin-faced, drooping-eyed man who was a tool of Reuben Slatt's by now and knew it all too well. He had to do what Slatt told him.

So it was that when Beth Adie came back from town with a buggy load of food, she was able to tell the Rebels that a reward was up for their capture.

'And it's in the name of the United States Government,' she said significantly, her manner saying they had gone too far now and she would have nothing to do with them. She was an ill-tempered girl these days, probably because Nameless wasn't having anything to do with her.

The reward offered one hundred dollars to anyone bringing in a Bandaged Man, dead or alive.

When that announcement was made Nameless looked around at his companions to see how they took it. He saw grim, unrelenting faces. Now they were proclaimed outlaws, outlawed by the government of the land, with a price upon their heads.

Joe Cullen said: 'We've got to do somethin' about that notice, but I ain't goin' back on what we started. Them skunks can't be left in control of our town no matter what it brings upon us in tryin' to kick 'em out!'

A growl of approval greeted his words. Nameless nodded. He had fighting men behind him and he was glad.

That evening marked another stage in the war upon those gunmen within the little cow town. A man with a rifle — a sharpshooter in the former army of the Confederacy — lying out on the mesquite, got the range on the saloon doors. A disgruntled gang found itself unable to get into the saloon except through back windows because of his unerring marksmanship.

There seemed a reluctance on the part of Slatt's men to ride out and rout the lone marksman. Probably they were uneasy, suspecting a trap. Perhaps they thought the marksman was there as a bait to bring them riding out of the town into some sort of ambush.

In the end, after a couple of hours' siege of the saloon, Reuben Slatt drove a dozen of his men out on horseback to put an end to the sniping. When he saw them coming the marksman rose and ran for a hidden horse. They saw his hideously-bandaged head and pulled away for a few hundred yards as if expecting to see more bandaged faces leap up at them out of the mesquite. That gave the marksman chance to get away.

Nameless was trying to look ahead and figure out their next move. He talked to his men in the bunkhouse, so that all knew what they were doing and were in agreement as to why they were doing it.

'Slatt's a bold man, though a mean hombre,' he kept warning his men. 'Ef he knows how few we are, he'll jump in to the attack. He'll send men relentlessly on our trail until we're all strung up or shot down. Right now, he doesn't know the size of the opposition, and he's playin' possum.'

Someone growled: 'I don't blame him. I reckon sight of our bandaged heads last night was enough to skeer any galoot! An' they wouldn't get a good count of us in the dark.'

Nameless was thinking hard. 'He mustn't ever get a good count of us,' he said. 'He must never know we're only a dozen agen his thirty-odd gunnies.'

Something made him lift his eyes. Beth Adie was standing in the doorway, listening to them. It was curious how

Beth always turned up at their conferences, listening and saying nothing — but missing nothing.

Nameless took his eyes away from her. He'd got an idea simmering in his mind and he wanted to put it across.

'What we've got to do is to convince Slatt that he hasn't a chance — that he's up agen more men than he's got, that if he don't get out of that town peaceably we'll be strong enough to kick him out!'

Joe Cullen said, helpfully: 'Let's know what's bitin' you, Nameless. You're on to somethin'. We want to know it.'

'We're goin' to let Reuben Slatt know that we've a darned sight more men than he's got,' Nameless said suddenly, and there was a big grin on his face. But more than that he wouldn't say at that moment.

But that night the Bandaged Men were in town again. Again they were lurking in the shadows, waiting for one of the gunmen to stray from the lighted area for just a moment.

Nameless wanted to go in and see Jeannie McNay, but there was no time for such diversions. And he wanted to go in especially and settle things with Tozer and Johnny Skulach, if they were still enjoying the hospitality of the McNays! He had his doubts about that, though. After last night they had probably hit the trail, wound or no wound, he thought grimly.

Not many men showed around the saloons that night. They were all inside but they didn't come walking the main street as they had done the previous night. Maybe they were uneasy about the Bandaged Men.

But in the end the Bandaged Men caught one staggering drunk, too filled with alcohol to have much caution left. The astonished man turned suddenly cold sober when hands gripped him from the darkness and his eyes saw those awful masks about him. A hand clapped across his mouth before a terrified scream could escape, and he was lifted off his feet and hastily bundled out of town.

Right on the edge of it was a lone dead tree. A rope had already been slung across it with a noose dangling uninvitingly at the height of a man's head. They got their prisoner and bound and gagged him and then stood him with his neck in that noose. But they didn't string him up. When that was done a horseman slowly walked out of the shadows and rode right across before the prisoner. The terrified eyes of that Border gunman saw the grim bandaged features look at him and then the horse went on into other shadows.

But now there was a second bandaged horseman grimly riding by, passing close before him, his slitted eyes looking balefully, menacingly at the man with his neck in the noose. And he rode on.

But as fast as a Bandaged Man rode out of sight there was another Bandaged Man to ride before him. For a full three minutes a procession of Bandaged Men paraded before the helpless man. Then the last of the Bandaged Men rode right up to the prisoner. Behind his gag the prisoner was trying to scream: 'Don't! Don't hang me! I don't want to die!'

But the last of the riders didn't even touch the rope that dangled behind the man's head. Instead he leaned from his saddle and pinned another note to the shirt of this quivering wretch.

The next thing there was a thundering roar as the Bandaged Men shot up the town. They raced their wild-eyed ponies down that moonlit main street, and when they came out at the far end there wasn't a pane of glass in any saloon or gaming establishment in Stampede. They were out and away on to the westward trail before any of Reuben Slatt's men really saw who had attacked them.

It wasn't until sunrise the following morning that Slatt found the Bandaged Men's prisoner slumped in his bonds beneath a tree out of town. The

Slatt men who saw that huddled figure approached cautiously, their eyes watching all the time for danger.

They turned their comrade over roughly, using their boot soles. They expected to find a corpse, but the prisoner's eyes rolled open and a light of gladness came to them as he recognised his comrades.

They released him and removed his gag and then took the note off the man's shirt. It said: 'This is the last warning. The next time we'll leave our prisoners kicking. Get out today or we'll lynch the lot of you!'

Again the signature was: 'The Bandaged Men.'

When Slatt spoke to the man who had been prisoner of the Bandaged Riders, he received news that startled him.

'We'd better git out, boss, while the goin's good,' the trembling man urged. He wiped sweat from his forehead, that had suddenly appeared as he remembered the previous night. 'I saw them ridin' past me, and there was dozens of 'em!'

'Dozens?'

'A mighty lot. I figure there was fifty or sixty of 'em if there was a dozen!'

Back on their bunks the Rebels wore smiles of contentment as they contemplated their night's work. Everything had gone off according to plan. Now, they were pretty sure, Reuben Slatt and his gang would be feeling mighty unhappy about their future.

Nameless came to sudden wakefulness with a bellow of alarm from their lookout man. Instantly there was confusion in that bunkhouse, as every man leapt to his feet and grabbed for guns and went pounding out through the doorway. Nameless led the way at a run into the high-walled compound. Their lookout man was up on the roof of the ranch-house itself.

He didn't need to shout down what had caused his alarm. They could hear hooves pounding along the trail towards them. After a time they realised it was one rider and he was coming in fast.

Nameless, listening intently, heard his men muttering: 'That'll be Dave!'

Dave was a sentry placed in an advanced position along the trail far out into the mesquite, to give them early warning if their enemies approached.

It was nearly dawn and though the moon was long since set there was a greying of the sky that told of the climbing morning sun.

They peered into the inevitable mists that always rolled in at this time of morning from the marshes, and suddenly from out of those wraith-like clouds a rider burst.

It was Dave. But he had someone on the saddle before him. Nameless leapt forward, anxiety gripping his heart.

It was Jeannie McNay.

She was lowered to the ground. The horse panted and tossed a foam-flecked head.

The men were shouting: 'What's wrong, Dave? Are them guys comin'?'

Dave shook his head behind the

bandages they always wore when on duty. They heard him growl: 'Nope, I didn't see nothin'. But Jeannie came walkin' in out of the night an' she wanted to see you in a hurry, Nameless. So I brought her.'

Nameless said: 'You did right. Now go back until the end of your watch.'

The rider obediently turned and cantered back along the trail towards Stampede. Nameless turned to Jeannie, his brow furrowed with anxiety.

Yet her first words were: 'For land's sake, Nameless, you tell your men not to wear bandages when I'm around! When I saw that head suddenly sticking out from behind a bush, I nearly fainted.'

The men laughed, relieved at her words, and yet she was serious enough. It must have been a shock, coming across a Bandaged Man out there in the early morning light on the lonely mesquite.

Nameless led the way to the bunk-house. He was shouting for coffee and breakfast for all of them, and men were running to get the stove stoked up. They went into the bunkhouse and sat at the table, Jeannie across from Nameless, an oil lamp lit over the doorway. She looked very tired.

Gently he said to her: ‘What brought you walkin’ the mesquite at this time of mornin’?’

She said, simply: ‘Johnny Skulach and Bully Tozer.’

The men standing round that table saw the knuckles of their leader go white as he clenched his fists. There was an omnious ring to his words as he asked: ‘What did they do? Tell me, Jeannie, an’ if they hurt you I’ll sure break their necks for them!’

Jeannie gulped. ‘They were getting mighty unpleasant,’ she admitted. ‘They’re not the kind of men to be cooped inside a house and not get up to mischief. I was the only one they could make a play for, and it got so that I couldn’t stand it any more. So I slipped out in the night and came across to see you.'

Nameless's jaw was set. 'They've got a nerve, stayin' on with you after what they tried to do to us!' His gesture embraced his grey-clad companions. 'I sure thought they would've lit out of town when Skulach saw his plan had come unstuck.'

Jeannie looked puzzled and clearly didn't know of Skulach's treachery. So Nameless told her about it.

'He tried to wipe us out. He wanted me to be wiped out, anyway. I beat him up, him and Tozer, back on an island in the swamp a little time ago. So when them Slatt's men were standin' outside the saloon he shouted to 'em, to draw attention upon us, hidin' in the shadows.'

He heard the quick intake of the girl's breath, and saw the leaping concern in her eyes to think of the narrow escape he had had, along with his companions, that eventful night.

'He thought I'd stop lead an' no one would ever know what he'd done, and he'd been left lyin' safely hidden in your home, Jeannie. That man sure is a mean hater!'

There was a snap in his voice that told of unpleasantness for the pair if ever he ran across them.

Jeannie said: 'I never knew about that.' Then she gripped his arm across the table. There was a shadow across them but neither turned. She said quickly: 'Nameless, they're tired of being cooped up there. I heard them talking late last night. They're planning to buy peace with their old gang again. They want to be out in that town, enjoying the saloons and the gambling. All they need is a bargaining counter so they can go to see Reuben Slatt.'

Nameless was watching her, sure that her shrewd mind held a greater knowledge than she had so far imparted. That shadow between them didn't move.

'They were talking about you, Nameless, you and your men. They must have heard something you said when you came to my room that night, and they're proposing to use it. They're just not sure they know enough yet.'

There was a curious silence in that roomful of men. For the first time that man and girl, intent upon each other, noticed it. Nameless looked round. His eyes lifted from the shadow.

It was thrown by Beth Adie's form, standing with her back to the lamp. And there was the most awful hatred on that face.

12

The moment his eyes alighted upon that raging face Nameless thought: 'This is the showdown! Now we're goin' to hit big trouble!'

He began to rise. Shaking with fury the girl pointed to Jeannie McNay and almost screamed: 'Take that girl out of my house. I won't have her in the place! Go on, get her out or I'll kill her!'

Old man Adie was in the bunkhouse now and he tried to interfere, but with an incredible strength his daughter threw him away. He wasn't the kind of man to go on interfering where his daughter's tantrums were concerned, and after that he kept out of it.

Then it was Nameless's turn. He received the full force of her temper. There was no love in those eyes now, only the deepest and vilest hatred.

She was a woman scorned. At any

rate, that was how she regarded herself. She had no chance to win this man, and now she hated herself for the way she had thrown herself at him publicly and been rejected.

She stormed at him: 'You get out, too! I won't have you in my house. You didn't tell me you were sneaking up to her room at nights — '

Nameless got angry at that. They saw the big fellow's eyes snap fire. He towered over Beth Adie, and shouted her down. He wasn't the kind of man to stand too much on niceties where a bad-tempered woman was concerned.

'You stop that sort of talk, Beth Adie! I never went to her room for anythin' wrong. But if that's the way you feel about it I ain't stayin' here. We'll both get out of the place.'

He looked round swiftly and saw the redheaded McNay boy. Grimly he said: 'You'd better come with us, too, or there'll be a lot worse talk comin' from this gal, I can see.'

He took hold of Jeannie by the hand

and began to propel her towards the door. He felt a resistance, as if Jeannie's fighting blood was up, as if she wanted to have a go at the furiously-angry Beth Adie herself.

But Nameless wasn't going to have any brawling. He took her by the shoulders and got her moving out into the early morning sunshine. He was saying to her: 'You forget what she had to say, Jeannie. Beth Adie means nothing to me.'

Then he heard the sneering voice of Beth from where she was standing by that rough plank table. 'And Jeannie McNay does?'

They both turned in the doorway. He looked down into Jeannie's face. She looked at him and both were asking a question. Then Jeannie smiled ever so slightly and nodded. Big Nameless's face relaxed a little at that and he smiled and nodded back, and the arm that was about her shoulders tightened quickly and told its own story.

The two faced the girl then, side by

side, resolutely standing together in the face of her vindictiveness.

'Sure, Jeannie means somethin' to my life,' he said, and there was a belligerence about his tone, a challenge, daring her to do her worst.

That filled the soul of Beth Adie with greater torment than she had ever known. Now she knew there was no chance whatever for her. If anything, she had driven them together by her anger and bad temper. But she wasn't going to let them remain together! If it was in her power to separate them, she was going to do so.

'If I can't have him, no one's going to have him,' she vowed.

She said, her voice unsteady with passion: 'You're forgetting one important thing, Nameless.'

The men were standing around silent, sensing the drama of this moment as that furious girl faced the pair in the doorway.

'Such as?'

'You're forgetting you're a nameless

man, a man without a past,' Beth said, and now her voice had sunk almost to a whisper. 'You don't know your past and you don't know what that past contains. But I'll tell you! You're married already! You won't ever have Jeannie McNay! There's a wife will be claiming you back in Houston the moment you set foot in that town!'

Nameless's arm dropped from Jeannie's shoulder. He gasped: 'Beth, what are you saying? How do you know all this?'

His bewildered eyes turned to look into Jeannie's shocked face. His hands spread out in appeal. 'I didn't know, Jeannie, honestly. A wife . . . ' His brow furrowed as if in pain as he tried desperately to go back into his memory to find at least confirmation for what Beth Adie was saying.

Jeannie seemed almost to jump forward, to take him by the shoulder and shake him roughly. It really was rough, he noticed. When he turned again to look at her it was to gaze into brown eyes that were blazing with indignation.

'Don't be a fool, Nameless! Don't swallow what that jealous little devil is saying to you!'

Helplessly he looked into Jeannie's animated face. 'You mean — ?'

'I mean she made that up out of sheer spite! She doesn't know anything about your past, I'll swear. Forget what she said, Nameless, and leave your past to find itself. We'll face up to those problems when we meet them.'

Nameless nodded agreement. And yet there was a lingering unhappiness in his eyes, because he wasn't sure. And if there was any truth in what Beth Adie had said to him, then he had no right to be trifling with this lovely girl's affections, no matter how sincere he felt at that moment.

Jeannie settled the matter by pulling him out through the doorway. But as they went, amid the uneasy stirrings of those unwitting, unwilling spectators, they heard Beth Adie's virulent voice call after them: 'I do know something about your past, Nameless. You'll find I know more than you think!'

* * *

Old Eb looked up as three riders came heading into the marshes towards him. He didn't bother to rise from where he was sitting against a doorpost in the early morning sunshine. He was whittling at a stick, but clearly he wasn't making anything — just passing away time.

The McNay boy got down, and then Nameless swung out of his saddle and let Jeannie slide down into his arms. He didn't hold her, though, didn't try to touch her in any way, and she understood.

Beth Adie's poison was having some effect. While there was doubt in Nameless's mind, he could not demonstrate his great liking for Jeannie. She didn't try to persuade him otherwise, appreciating what was in his thoughts.

But they were two unhappy people as they came across to where old Eb was cutting shavings.

They said: 'Howdy,' to old Eb, who found enough words to answer back.

'Howdy, folks.'

And then he was silent for a while.

They sat around for a little time, while Nameless explained the situation to Eb. 'We're gonna live with you for a few days, Eb. You don't mind ef we leave our blanket rolls here?'

Eb didn't mind. He shook his head and went on whittling. So Nameless said: 'We'll be sleeping here nights, we three. Right now, though, Red an' me have got work to do outside. So I'm leavin' Jeannie in your care. Think you can look after her?'

For the first time old Eb gave evidence of a sense of humour. He glanced up at that fine big girl and said slowly: 'I figger Jeannie c'n mebbe look after me instead.'

They said goodbye to the girl, leaving her with a gun as a means of protection. Old Eb shook his head at that gun. He didn't believe in 'em. But the others did, especially when there were skunks like Tozer and Skulach and the Reuben Slatt gang about.

They rode on to the mesquite in front of the Adie spread and the rest of their followers rode out to join them. It was better that the Rebels stayed on at the Adie house, Nameless thought, in spite of the fact that it was annoying to have their forces split at this critical time.

The two men who had stopped lead a couple of nights ago remained behind, so eleven of them took the trail that morning.

They were not letting up on their reign of terror over the Slatt gang. It was essential that while the mob thought themselves outnumbered the Bandaged Men struck at every opportunity.

Nameless intended to strike that day. He had an idea. He rode north with his men to the main trail into Stampede, and they camped across that road for most of the day. Around sunset a small party of men came galloping down the trail. There were five of them.

Five startled riders came to a sudden halt as a horseman slowly paced his mount across the trail. The jaws of those unshaven, ragged Border scum dropped blankly open as they looked upon that horseman — a grey-clad, Confederate-uniformed rider, but with a difference. A man without a head! At least a man whose head was completely obscured by the turns of a broad bandage.

The grim, ghastly rider turned his horse's head to face the five startled scallawags. As he did so other Bandaged Men started to come out from the cover of the rocks by the side of the trail and range themselves alongside their companion.

One of the quintet suddenly rasped out an oath and remembered to go for his gun, but his hand halted inches from the butt of a Colt. For upon that move ten guns like lightning flashed into the hands of those masked men, and all the barrels converged on that one angry scallawag. He stopped being angry. He lifted his hands more than shoulder high, so quickly he nearly dislocated his collar bone. The other men with him didn't try any tricks but lifted their hands, too.

One of the riders — a man now seen to be wearing a blue shirt above his Rebel-grey pants, pushed his horse up among those ragged riders. A voice like raw steel asked a question of the nearest: 'You thought you were goin' to join Reuben Slatt, didn't you?'

The sullen-faced gunman resorted to temper and snarled: 'Who says? An' what's it got to do with you?'

He so far forgot himself as to lower his arms as if to strike out at that Bandaged Man. The next moment a hand gripped his shoulder and there was a sickening pain as skilful leverage was applied. The scallawag crashed out of his saddle into the dust. He lay there in pain, trying to recover his breath.

The Bandaged Man with the blue shirt surveyed the others. 'Anyone else like to get down from his saddle?' he asked softly. Something like a chuckle went up from one of those other grim-visaged figures. Then they were all silent and menacing and seemingly inhuman again.

'You fellars git down,' was the sudden order.

With poor grace the men dismounted, just as their companion found breath enough to stagger again to his feet.

Blue Shirt gave more orders. He seemed the kind of man who could give orders all the time, those unhappy men were thinking. Here they had been on their way to what had promised to be something right in their line. Slatt's message, in calling them in to join him, had told of a whole town at the mercy of scallawags, a town where there were rich pickings for unscrupulous rogues.

They had been hastening there, full

of joy, and now they had run into this bunch of men, the like of which they had never seen in their lives before. Even before Blue Shirt spoke they had a feeling that this was an end to that promised bonanza where liquor was free and no one had to work for money.

Blue Shirt confirmed it with his orders. 'You ain't goin' anywhere near that town. Any man I see tryin' to make Stampede will git himself hanged from the highest tree around these parts.'

That voice sent a chill into those men, for they realised that Blue Shirt was not joking. He meant every word of it.

'We're collectin' hosses. You don't need them as much as we do. You're goin' to walk back the way you came, an' if you meet any scum like yourselves on the trail you'd better tell 'em to turn back because we'll be waitin' for 'em.

'Now unbuckle your belts and step out of 'em. We're also collectin' guns an' ammunition.'

The five men sullenly let their

cartridge belts and holstered guns drop into the dust. Obedient under the threat of those menacing guns they stepped away from their weapons.

They all started to turn, to walk back up the trail, but Blue Shirt ordered one of them back. It was the ruffian whom he had hurled from his saddle.

'Nope, fellar, you ain't goin' back that way.' Blue Shirt's voice was very soft but nonetheless unpleasant. 'Brother, you're goin' into Stampede with a message. You other fellars, git goin' now!'

The other Bandaged Men drove the four sullen, protesting scamps along the trail, starting them on the long and weary walk back to the next town northwards. They didn't like the idea of that long hike, but there was no arguing against guns.

The man they had left behind looked suddenly sick at being separated from his companions. His cheeks went pale under the black whiskers that grew profusely upon his face. He looked wistfully after his companions — he would even have preferred that long walk northwards just so long as he had company.

For he was afraid for himself if he went into Stampede alone. They had been told to bring horses and guns, and he would be of no value to Reuben Slatt without either.

He had none . . . he had even less, a few minutes later.

When the other four scallawags were well up the trail, one of the Bandaged Men dismounted and walked over to their remaining prisoner. He fingered the man's shirt.

'Reckon it ain't clean, but it'd wash. Off with it, fellar, I'm startin' collectin' shirts.'

Protesting, they hauled the shirt off their prisoner. That done there was another Bandaged Man there looking him over.

He shook his head. The slitted eyes through that bandage were staring down at that prisoner's pants. 'Ain't much good. Reckon they wouldn't last, but they'd come in mighty handy for a change.'

That hideous bandaged head lifted and the prisoner quailed before the grim eyes that peered out at him.

'I'm collectin' pants, fellar. You git out of them quick!'

A howl went up from the prisoner and he tried to appeal to the other Bandaged Men, but they watched him in stony and menacing silence. He came out of his pants in a hurry.

Then another Bandaged Man was standing before him, looking at him, naked save for the boots on his feet.

The bandaged head shook sadly. 'You ought to be ashamed of yourself, wearin' boots like that. They ain't fit to be worn.'

Then he looked down at his own boots, showing under the grey uniform trousers.

'All the same,' the Bandaged Man sighed, 'they look better than mine. Reckon I'd better start collectin' boots.

You won't need 'em, fellar. You ain't more'n five miles to go. That won't hurt your bare feet none. Come on, jump out of them boots!'

And jump out that prisoner did, too. When he was completely naked on the trail, Blue Shirt said: 'Now, you go find Reuben Slatt and tell him he won't get no more reinforcements into Stampede. Tell him we've got men watching every trail into the town and we're gonna turn back any scamps like yourself who think they're gonna fight for Slatt.

'An' give him one final message. Ef he don't get out of Stampede pronto we'll come in an' drive him out. Tell him we're being kind to him because we don't want to have a fight in Stampede that might hurt innocent people. But that's our last warning. Ef Slatt doesn't pull out with his men right away, we'll strike — hard!'

The man mightn't have understood all that was being said to him, but when he was told to get moving along that trail he did so with alacrity. It looked mighty unhealthy to stay there with those Bandaged Men, naked or not naked.

Ten Bandaged Men grinned as they watched that naked man start reluctantly upon the long limp into Stampede.

Suddenly, upon a signal from Blue Shirt, every horse whirled in a cloud of dust and disappeared off the trail. The naked man shook his fist after them, but that did no good. So then he began once again to make his way along that hot, dusty trail to pass on the bandaged leader's message to Reuben Slatt.

Slatt did not leave Stampede.

Bandaged Men were watching the town, and they rode in to report to Nameless, out in the swamps with Jeannie McNay and old Eb and some other Bandaged Men off duty.

'Nobody's lit out of Stampede since old barefoot Johnny got in,' Joe Cullen reported. 'I told you Reuben Slatt's got guts and he ain't to be skeered by no words.'

Nameless rose, throwing away the stick he had been idly whittling, in imitation of Eb.

'Then we'll drive 'em out,' he rasped. 'Call the boys. Tonight we're gonna ride. Tonight we'll put the fear of death into those men. We'll force 'em out, some way. And they won't know that we're only a dozen men, agen their thirty odd!'

⋆ ⋆ ⋆

After sunset a nervous township suddenly saw a bright glow to the south of them. The glow brightened rapidly, and all at once there was an island of flame half a mile to the south of them — as if light had been set to piles of brushwood.

Suddenly, when the fire was at its highest, the black shape of a silhouetted horseman slowly paced his way in front of the flames.

He had almost come to the end of the fiery barrier when a second rider slowly paced his way after him. And after that rider came a third and a fourth and a fifth . . .

The men under Slatt gasped as they counted. 'Forty,' someone suddenly said. There was panic in his voice. 'And still they come!'

The men were watching from the verandahs of the various saloons, all so intent on that blood-chilling procession of riders that they were not even looking to a possible danger from their rear.

It was then that the masked riders struck.

Nameless had led his men into the town while the attention of the Slatt gang was distracted by that fiery diversion to the south of Stampede. It was two wounded men, had Slatt only known it, playing their part magnificently. They were leading five spare horses upon which dummies had been carefully fixed, and the wounded men were parading them round and round in front of that fire as if there was an army of them instead of — just two.

Nameless dismounted, and leaving the horses in the care of two of his men he led the other eight stealthily along the rear of the saloons and gaming places. Once they heard the rumble of wheels as a vehicle came into the town, and then they froze, not sure whether it might turn down one of the alleys and run into them. They could not afford to be seen. They were heavily outnumbered and surprise was their best weapon.

They gained the rear of the principal saloon; the saloon that had been owned by an uncle of Jeannie McNay until recently. Now it was Reuben Slatt's.

Nameless slowly lifted his bandaged head to peer into one of the back windows. He saw a saloon completely deserted, with every man out on the rails overlooking the street. Even the new proprietor and the barmen were out of the room. Swiftly and silently Nameless slipped around and opened a side door into the saloon. The other men followed, their guns drawn, ready for action.

Like great, creeping cats they stole softly down that big room, their shadows moving with them in the light from the oil lamps.

Still the men out front were occupied with the fiery spectacle to the south of the town. They were leaning against the rails, oblivious of the movement behind them.

About half-a-dozen gunnies were on the verandah, standing with their feet up on the verandah rail. Most other men had descended into the street, to get an uninterrupted view of the conflagration.

Nameless walked boldly out on to the verandah, though his bandaged head could have been seen quite clearly if any of the men had turned. He took up his position behind one of the scallawags standing against that rail. Nameless's other men silently stole out and stationed themselves behind the men on the verandah. Then eight bandaged heads turned to look at their leader, awaiting a signal.

It was slow in coming. They looked at their leader in surprise. He seemed to have forgotten the mission in hand. Then their eyes turned to follow the direction in which he was looking.

There was a buggy along the street, just a few yards away. It was like any other buggy, and yet all those men felt that it looked familiar.

But Nameless was watching something else. Behind that buggy someone was standing at a door that was only partly open. It was hard to distinguish details in the shadows, but Nameless was sure it was a girl who was standing there.

And he was sure it was Beth Adie.

Under his bandage he licked his lips at the thought and his eyes were grim. For the only person Beth Adie could be talking to across at that house would be Johnny Skulach!

Nameless worked it out in that moment. Beth had come into town on purpose to speak with Johnny Skulach. He knew instinctively that this meant treachery. That Beth Adie was working against them.

Under his bandages he swore to himself. Beth with her insane jealousy couldn't forgive him because he preferred Jeannie McNay to herself. And because she could not forgive it was apparent she was out to punish.

A man turned, right in front of Nameless.

Nameless saw a face crack open and eyes almost leap out of the man's head as he looked upon that line of silent Bandaged Men standing against the saloon wall.

Nameless picked him up by the ears and hurled him through the batwings into the saloon. It was the signal.

Every man on that verandah suddenly found himself gripped and tumbled backwards inside the saloon. The noise brought heads round to see what was happening.

The Bandaged Men were leaping for

cover now, diving after their prisoners inside the saloon. On the street the scallawags recognised the Bandaged Men and a mighty shout went up. Instantly the mob in the street began to scatter, their guns coming out, flames spurting towards the saloon.

The Bandaged Men hurled themselves on to the floor and stabbed back with their guns.

Their six prisoners were being disarmed hastily and then shoved roughly towards the back door. Four men were hustling them out, while six men and their blue-shirted leader jumped to the door and windows and opened fire on the mob in the street. Reuben Slatt was out there, somewhere in the darkness, his voice roaring orders. He was trying to drive his men into the attack.

Nameless got his guns stammering, and men wilted away before him. But then the attack came back. Slatt had too many followers, and when they opened up, their heavy bullets almost tore the frail saloon woodwork into splinters.

The prisoners had started to fight, made reckless by the thought that they were being carried off as prisoners of these sinister Bandaged Men.

Nameless was roaring above the shouting and the shooting, but nobody seemed to know what he was saying in that din.

So he jumped across and lashed out among the prisoners, driving them before his ferocious attack down the steps and into the darkness beyond. All the Bandaged Men raced out of the saloon and encircled their prisoners at once.

The Bandaged Men were fighting a savage rearguard action, hustling their prisoners across towards the horses.

Slatt came looming up out of the darkness, his gun stabbing savagely towards the crouching ring of Bandaged Men. He had guts, that ruffian leader, and he led a charge upon the masked men.

But by this time the prisoners were being slung on to horses, with masked men leaping up behind to cover them with guns stuck into their ribs.

Horses were screaming and plunging at their bridles, but then they were released and immediately started to race away into the darkness. Nameless and his rearguard were there to fight back at the threatening Slatt's mob, and for a few vicious minutes they fought a noisy gun battle.

Then somehow all the Bandaged Men had found their horses and had climbed into their saddles and gone plunging out towards the darkness.

Their leader was last to go. He leapt into his saddle with both guns flaring, fighting to keep back these men who threatened his followers.

They had a savage fight to get out of the town. Reuben Slatt was raving at his followers to cut down these interlopers, and he had sent his gunmen running into the alleys to head them off.

Somehow a lamp must have got

knocked over, and a building started to go up in flames, and the lurid red glow made those mounted Bandaged Men look even more ghastly and frightening than ever.

The prisoners were up before the masked men, to some extent serving as unwilling shields against the gunfire of their ruffianly companions. They didn't like it, and they were shouting from the saddles to Reuben Slatt to hold off with his guns.

An indescribable scene of confusion existed for minutes. Horses reared, even though loaded with double burdens, as guns blatted right under their noses. The Bandaged Men were cursing under their tasks, fighting savagely, firing until their guns were empty, and then reversing them and using the butts as clubs.

Big Nameless was right in the midst of all the fighting, beating down upon their opponents and forcing a pathway into safety.

And then all at once they were

through. They were in darkness, and the night gave them cover and safety.

They rode five miles or so into the mesquite and then disposed of the prisoners.

The men were set on the ground. A few lost their shirts — good ones they had filched from the stores in Stampede — in the process. And then they were addressed by Nameless himself.

'Keep walking. Ef you turn to head back towards Stampede we'll shoot you out of hand. We're givin' you a chance to save your lives. Take it, brothers.'

They saw those cursing, shuffling men head away from them into the darkness. Nameless had a feeling they would only circle and go back into Stampede, but this was the best they could do to disturb their enemies. If these men did take fright and go away from Reuben Slatt, then their night's work had been most effective. Slatt would be without a few of his gunmen and the odds against the Bandaged Men would be more nearly equal.

That disposed of, Nameless put spurs into his horse and almost flogged it all the way back to the Adie homestead. His men couldn't understand it. They didn't see the need for hurry.

Joe Cullen voiced their feelings. 'What's the hurry, big fellar?' They were riding low in their saddles, neck to neck, risking injury in that darkness which showed the trail only as a faint grey ribbon under the starlit sky.

Nameless said: 'I'll tell you when we get to the Adie place. But not before.'

His voice was grim. When they got to the Adie ranch, old man Adie came out with a lamp to greet them. He was saying something about the wounded men who had returned with those dummies that had been used on their spare horses. They had gone into the marshes, he said, to Jeannie McNay to have their wounds attended to.

Dismounting, Nameless heard the old man in silence. Then he shot a question at him. 'They had to go to Jeannie McNay for attention? That means that Beth ain't here?'

The old man looked puzzled. 'Nope, she ain't. Must've gone out some time this evening.' He looked uneasy. 'A gal shouldn't go around like that, I know, but I ain't got no control over her.'

And then he said, as if to console himself: 'She'll be back soon, I reckon.'

But Nameless was shaking his head. He didn't want to hurt the old man, but he said: 'Nope, old-timer, I don't reckon she will be back.'

He was remembering how she had been furtively speaking with men who could only be enemies of theirs, and that meant that Beth Adie had thrown in her hand with the enemy.

Suddenly Nameless couldn't hang around that Adie ranch any longer. He told his men to look after themselves and make themselves comfortable. He was going straight for the marshes, even though the night's darkness made such a journey hazardous.

He wanted to see Jeannie McNay. He couldn't understand how Beth Adie's treachery might affect him, but he was shrewd enough to know that Jeannie would solve the puzzle.

Jeannie was a woman and would know how a woman's mind worked. She would be able to say why Beth had gone to Johnny Skulach. If he knew that he would know where to look for danger.

* * *

The girl was awake. She was dressing the shoulder wound of one of the boys by the light of the fire. The other had already been attended to and was curled up asleep. Eb was nowhere to be seen. That wasn't surprising. Eb was a law unto himself.

They were glad to see him. Jeannie was pleased and didn't bother to hide it. She said: 'I didn't expect to see you tonight, Nameless. But you're welcome, right welcome.' And she started to make coffee and rustle up some food for him.

He let her busy herself about the fire, while the other soldier went to join his companion in sleep. Nameless watched the girl with an ache in his heart. Every time he looked at her he was reminded of his past. Or reminded that he was a man with no past.

She caught his expression. She smiled. She knew what was in his mind. 'The worst might never happen,' she said.

'The worst could happen,' he said, and she probably knew what he meant. He sighed and quickly turned the conversation.

'Jeannie, I want your help. Thar's somethin' happenin' and I can't make head nor tail of it. I think Beth Adie's gone over to the enemy.'

She looked up at that, quickly, and saw the grim lines etched into that young brown face. Such a good face, she was thinking, and her heart smote her because she knew there was a barrier between them — a barrier caused by a memory that couldn't cling to the past.

'I saw Beth Adie in town tonight. She was whisperin' to Johnny Skulach at your old place. I reckon she wasn't there to help us!'

Jeannie took the coffee pot off as it started to boil over, and nodded her head. 'So, I reckon she was plannin' to hurt us.'

Jeannie didn't pretend. 'She wants you, Nameless, and when she knew you'd been to my place she hated you because she felt you were lost to her.'

Suddenly Jeannie smiled. It was a nice smile. And she was so frank. She said: 'I don't blame her for wanting you so much.'

Nameless squatted on his heels beside the girl at the fire. There was an agony on his face, a tumult within him . . . A tumult of emotion that was so great he could not find expression in his limited vocabulary.

There was strain in his voice as he

said: 'Jeannie, I haven't known you long. But I reckon you know how I feel about you. I've felt like this since I first clapped eyes on you.'

She was still smiling. She reached out and took his hand. She said, simply: 'I'm glad. Yes, I've known.'

He sighed. 'This makes things hard. I mean, knowing how you feel about me, and me feeling like I do.' He was groping in his mind for words to express himself, but the agony in his eyes told the story better. 'I reckon, though, in fairness to you, Jeannie, we didn't ought to get this goin' any deeper. You don't know what's waitin' for me round the corner.'

She said: 'We don't. Mebbe there's some reason why we might never be able to come together if you remember your past, but that dosn't matter, Nameless. It's been . . . so nice to know a man like you!'

They sat there for a while, holding hands by the fireside. The mist was drifting in, rising from the sluggish waters of the marshland as the cool night wind swept silently over the sun-warmed waters.

In the end, however, Nameless sighed. He smiled at her. 'Reckon I forgot what I came about.'

'Beth Adie?'

He nodded. 'Sure. I came to hear you tell me what she was plannin' with Skulach. I can't make things fit, somehow.'

'It's plain — as plain as anything I've ever known,' Jeannie said with assurance. 'Remember what I told you about Skulach. He was regretting his fight with Reuben Slatt. He didn't like to be hiding like a sick dog in our house. He wanted to be out, sharing the spoils of the town and drinking and having a good time with his old comrades. I told you that Skulach was trying to think out some good excuse for going back to Reuben Slatt, something that would give him protection if he did show his face before his old gang leader. Well, Nameless, don't you see, Beth Adie's gone and given him his excuse.'

'You mean — ?'

'Beth Adie's told Skulach all about you, including the smallness of your numbers and the fact that your men are hiding out on the Adie ranch. Skulach can trade that information for safety. I bet right now he's telling Reuben Slatt what he knows about you, and I'll bet the whole gang will be riding on the Adie ranch before sun-up.'

Nameless rose, cursing Beth Adie under his breath. She had spoilt their plans just when they were beginning to be successful! Just two or three more raids and the Slatt gang would be so depleted they would be fighting on even terms.

But if Jeannie was right — and in his heart he knew she was — it put an end to their schemes. The Bandaged Men would not be terrifying any more. Reuben Slatt would be riding to wipe them out on sight.

Nameless said, grimly: 'I hope I don't come across Beth Adie ever again. It's not just me she's punishin', it's all her friends — including the people she knows in Stampede. She's put a whole town back in the grip of them blamed scallawags!'

He went across to his horse.

Jeannie rose and asked quickly: 'Where are you going?'

'Back to the Adie spread. I reckon I'd better bring the boys back here.'

Jeannie walked with him to the edge of the causeway, Nameless leading his horse. She said, softly: 'Skulach knows the way into these marshes. Bringing those boys here might be bringing them into a trap.'

'Mebbe. But these marshes might come in useful. Leastways, there's no place else we can hide out close to Stampede and be useful. I figger we'll ride back here, even if only to make one stand agen them gunnin' devils!'

She said: 'Goodbye.'

He hesitated, wanting to take her in his arms and kiss her, and he knew she wanted it, too. But then he turned away.

That wasn't going to help. If ever his memory came back and he found that he had kissed some other girl before and married her . . .

Jeannie called to him. He heard her say unexpectedly: 'Nameless, there's men at work on the railroad. They're away back beyond the hills, getting the track ready for use again.'

He paused, trying to understand the implication of her words. Clearly she was connecting this railroad with his past. Clearly she felt that the entry of these railroad workers into the district might assist him in some way. He shrugged.

'What of it?' — wearily. 'That don't seem of any importance now at all.'

The only thing that was important was the safety of his comrades and the ultimate success of their plans to defeat Reuben Slatt and his domineering, brutal gang.

The moon helped him along that misty causeway that was only inches higher than the deadly swamps wherein lurked water snakes and alligators and other reptiles from a more primitive era. As he went he peered for a sign of old Eb. He was puzzled. Eb didn't usually stray away from his fire late at night. He wondered if the old man had come to harm, and he remembered his frailness and the bad time he had had at the hands of Skulach and Bully Tozer.

But Eb wasn't to be seen, and out on dry land Nameless mounted his horse and picked his way across the mesquite towards the Adie ranch.

As he went he thought grimly of Skulach and Tozer. It was the inconsistency of behaviour on the part of the two men. Both were bullies. Both were cowards. Both were evil men without thoughts of loyalty or comradeship in their minds.

Certainly there was none in Skulach's selfish life for anyone at all. And yet Bully Tozer, the stronger of the two, and capable of defeating Skulach in any physical encounter — Tozer allowed himself to be bullied and bossed about by his weaker companion. It had puzzled Nameless before. Now that he thought of it again he was mystified.

'I figger Skulach must have some hold over Tozer,' he thought. But then he dismissed the idea. Tozer wasn't the kind of man to behave as he did simply because someone had some sort of hold over him.

Nameless dismissed the thought from his mind. He forgot about it completely, because ahead of him he saw light and he knew it must come from the Adie ranch.

He rode into a trap.

13

The moon was showing fitfully between ragged clouds that told of an approaching storm. It wasn't a big moon, either, and it meant that most of the time Nameless rode with his head down, his eyes peering uncertainly into the gloom.

When he was near the Adie ranch, the moon for a few moments came out fully. There was more light than he'd had on any part of the journey before. He was trying to distinguish the low buildings with its background of trees when he realised that he was not alone.

In fact, he had walked his horse right in among other riders. They must have realised that he was a stranger almost as quickly as he had detected danger. He wasn't wearing his bandage, and there was enough light for them to see his face — and it wasn't one of the faces of their comrades, those other mounted men knew!

The mesquite had been silent until that moment, silent save for that rustling, stirring night wind. But in a fraction of a second all that was changed.

There was a hoarse shout that suddenly rang out. Instantly all was confusion. Men dragged round on their horses' heads, and there was the flash of light on gun metal. Added to the scream of suddenly-spurred horses came a swelling, angry chorus from those night riders.

Someone fired. Nameless had his gun out and opened up immediately. Desperately he sent his horse plunging right through that line of horsemen. In his brain hammered the words: 'Reuben Slatt! He's here with his gang already!'

Unwittingly in the dark he had stumbled upon the Slatt mob ready to make a surprise attack on the Adie place!

He went through that surprised line

of men, his guns flaring redly in the darkness, carving out a pathway for himself and his horse. Lead screamed hatefully past him and he lay low along the neck of his horse, urging it to frantic speed.

The fight was over in a matter of seconds, because he had that second's advantage over the Slatt gang which gave him a tiny lead. A very small lead but sufficient to enable him to lose himself in the darkness of that shadowy mesquite.

Recklessly now he spurred on, heading as fast as he could towards the ranch. He knew the gunfire would have alarmed his followers, and as he saw the high compound wall looming up towards him he came in shouting: 'Git your hosses! The Slatt gang's comin'!'

He didn't ride through the gates of the compound. That might have been putting himself in a trap. He saw a bandaged face up at the wall, and then the man was down.

Already he heard the jingling of

harness metal in the darkness before the house. No doubt at the sound of firing the men had immediately dived for their horses.

Nameless wheeled, his guns pointing into the dark mesquite, covering that gateway against attack. He peered out, ready to blast off at first sight of the enemy.

Then he heard the Slatt gang thundering up. They were coming in force now, and it would only be a matter of seconds before they were up to the ranch and surrounding it. Nameless wanted to be out of the place before that happened.

He heard horses' hooves from behind him and knew that the first of his riders was racing out of the compound.

Then he saw shadows, the shadows of Slatt's men charging in from the darkened mesquite.

He wheeled his horse and sent it plunging for the deepest shadows.

There was a rattle of gunfire from behind him, and a quiver ran through his horse and he knew it had been shot. Desperately he urged the dying beast along for a few more strides. His horse crashed down.

Nameless kicked free from his stirrups as he felt himself falling and hit the earth at a run. He kept on running, stumbling through the mesquite and the clinging thorns of the scrub that tried to pull him back.

He must have gained the lead he needed, because by the sounds behind him those Slatt men hadn't seen him come off his horse. He kept on running. The moon partly dimmed as a haze of clouds drifted before it.

Nameless heard a shout and knew that his stricken horse had been seen. Now they would come hunting for him systematically, aiming to rout out the man on foot.

All at once he got the smell of sweating horseflesh. Before he knew what he was doing he had run up against a horse . . . two horses.

There was a wheel showing where

moonlight reflected on a burnished steel rim. He knew what it was.

A buggy.

There was a little cry of alarm from the high seat. A girl's voice. Nameless spun round and dived for it. He saw Beth's face in that moonlight. She saw him and there was panic on it.

There was no time for niceties. He grabbed for Beth, dragging her clean out of her seat. She was trying to scream, trying, he knew, to give warning to the enemy.

Nameless clapped his hand over her mouth. He didn't do it gently. His life was at stake and this girl was responsible.

He hissed into her ear: 'Shut your mouth! You brought this on yourself, an' I ain't gonna let you give me up to your new friends!'

She bit his fingers. He grabbed her by the throat, not painfully, but sufficient for her to know that he wouldn't stand for any more tricks.

She was panting in terror, but then

her native cunning quickly asserted itself. As he stood listening to the sound of the search not very far away he heard her whisper: 'You'll never get away alive, Nameless!'

He said nothing. He had nothing to say. He was still listening, trying to determine the whereabouts of his searchers. They seemed pretty well all around him.

She whispered again: 'You'll never get away, you or your followers! Why don't you see that?'

Still he didn't answer. He was seeing a way out of this trap into which he had unwittingly stumbled.

She tried again. Softly: 'Slatt will soon have an army of men at his call. There'll be hundreds after you, and I don't care where you hide, if you're in this district they'll dig you out!'

An army of men . . .

Nameless couldn't understand what she meant. What army of men could possibly be recruited locally to fight against these Confederates? There weren't that many traitors in the South, he thought grimly. Only Beth Adie had turned against them so far.

There was anger in his voice as he growled: 'What are you suggestin'? That I run out on my friends now, while I've chance?'

She was eager. 'We could slip away on the buggy, Nameless. We could be out of the county before daylight. You'd be safe!'

'And my friends would be trapped inside the quags!' They would be if Slatt *could* call upon an army of men. He felt in his heart that there was truth in Beth's statement, that in some mysterious way Slatt had acquired countless allies.

He shook her, his rage suddenly almost overpowering. 'That would be treachery,' he growled. 'Ef my friends are to die in the quags, I'm gonna be with them!'

Saying which Beth found herself hurled roughly into the dried scrub. In that same second Nameless had leapt into the driving seat of the buggy and was lashing the horses into activity.

Beth began to scream.

He stood on the footboard, lashing the horses with the long whip that had been in its stand. He couldn't see more than a few yards ahead of the horses, and he relied on their instinct to keep him away from danger.

All he knew was the general direction in which the quags lay, and he headed that way.

There was firing, stabbing jets of orange and red from the mesquite. Lead began to scream across towards him, but he went on without so much as ducking to avoid it. They wouldn't hit him except with a lucky shot in that darkness, he thought grimly.

The Slatt men had got the sound of those rolling wheels, and he heard the thunder of hooves that grew louder as they got on to his trail. They could travel faster across this trackless mesquite than a buggy, he knew.

He wasn't far from the quags now,

and tugging on a rein to get the horses swerving, he took a flying leap into the bushes.

Crouching, he saw the buggy career away into the darkness. A few seconds later men burst out from the night, lying low in their saddles, following the sound of that receding vehicle.

In a matter of seconds the whole mob had streamed past. Then Nameless rose to his feet and began to run. It took him half an hour to find the way into the quags.

A tiny, shielded fire threw a red glow on the faces of his companions. He told them the situation.

'We might be trapped here. Mebbe it would be a good thing if we got out of this place now, while we've got a chance.'

Joe Cullen looked surprised. 'Trapped? We ain't as many as the Slatt mob, but they'll never dig us out of these swamps! We can hold our own for a long time — mebbe for all time!'

So Nameless told them what Beth

Adie had said. 'She talked of an army of men comin' to the help of Reuben Slatt.'

The men whistled in surprise. They were as baffled as Nameless about these new additions to Slatt's force.

'Where in Hades can Slatt be findin' men?'

It was Jeannie McNay's brother exclaiming in surprise. 'I reckon that was bluff, Nameless! I reckon we've got nothin' to fear more than Reuben Slatt an' his hoodlums. I'm goin' to sleep. We can take on the Slatt mob tomorrow when it's daylight.'

'Daylight? That's any time now. Then,' Nameless said grimly, 'we'll know if Beth was bluffin' or not.'

Instinctively he knew there was no bluff. He knew that army would be standing silently outside the swampland, possibly right then, waiting for dawn and a chance to attack.

When the first grey light began to filter through that swirling swamp mist, Nameless went back along the causeway with several others. They came upon their two sentries, crouching at the end of the causeway, where the mesquite took over.

The men raised themselves from the damp grass in which they were lying. They had put their bandages on. Nameless and the others were without their masks, though, Nameless had told his men to put them on if there was to be action. It gave a slight advantage, he thought, to look so fiercesome with their bandaged heads. It also enabled them to identify their own men in the heat of battle.

One of the sentries whispered through his bandages: 'They're out there. We've been hearin' voices this last hour. A lot of men.'

'A lot?' The others stared uneasily down at the shadowy figure of the sentry.

'A mighty lot. Listen!'

They listened. Through the mist that was lifting rapidly in the warming rays of the morning sun, they heard the sounds of men in the distance. As the sentry said, there seemed to be a mighty lot out there on the mesquite.

In the curious way that happened every morning, all at once the mists seemed to lift and the sun shone through. Revealed in that golden morning light they saw out on to the mesquite. Their eyes straining through the last shredding drifts of mist, Nameless and the Rebels stared out to see what peril the morning brought them.

They saw a good two hundred men waiting out there for this moment when they could see to advance into the swamp.

They saw mounted men who would be Reuben Slatt's. But with them was a great milling mob of men on foot.

They were too far away to be identified.

The Rebels clustered together for a hurried council of war.

'I reckon they'll dig us out of this swampland in time,' said Nameless. 'I reckon we should git away from these quags as quick as we can.'

'You know another way out?'

'Yeah, Joe. I know another way out.' There was movement from those mounted men on the mesquite. They were coming forward. The attack was about to begin! 'I reckon we should git out that way as soon as we can.'

He made up his mind. 'Fight on the retreat,' he told them. 'Fall back, but don't let 'em come in with a rush. Make it slow.

'I'm goin' to get Jeannie out, so that she doesn't get mixed up in this business. When she's clear, we'll all slip out the back way I know.'

'Won't anyone else know that way out?' Nameless knew what was in Cullen's mind. Maybe already more of their enemies would be watching that other track out from the swamps.

'Mebbe. It's somethin' we'll find out very soon!'

Nameless's voice was grim. He thought again of old Eb. Old Eb wouldn't admit it but Nameless was prepared to bet the old man knew a dozen ways out of this swamp. But old Eb seemed to have disappeared. Nameless frowned, thinking about it. He wondered if any harm had come to the old man.

The horde of Slatt men came pouring in towards the causeway. Quite distinctly now Nameless could see Johnny Skulach riding alongside the red-faced, evil-looking gang leader, Reuben Slatt.

Nameless found himself snarling with impotent rage. If he only had a rifle right then he would have put a bullet into the worthless, treacherous Johnny Skulach! But he hadn't a rifle. And time was pressing. He began to put on his bandage.

With a swift last word of encouragement to his men, Nameless turned and began to race back along that causeway. Now he was able to move with speed, because he could see the way quite clearly.

He was half-way back to the camp when he heard the rattle of gunfire behind him. Reuben Slatt, with his overwhelming force, had begun the attack on the men trapped within the quagmire.

When Nameless reached the camp he found the others all up and waiting for him. Jeannie came running to meet him, her face concerned.

He called his men together and told them of the situation at the end of the causeway. 'We're in a tough spot. Somewhere, somehow, Slatt has got himself a mighty army of helpers. We've got to get out of these quags. Now there's no question of being able to hold out agen Slatt!'

He told Jeannie to get on to a horse. Then he mounted himself.

'I'm takin' Jeannie out along another pathway,' he told his men. 'You've got to give her a chance — fight on the retreat and hold back Slatt as long as you can. Ef that other pathway's clear, we can all get out sooner or later. But fight hard — don't let Slatt overrun you. I'll be back!'

His men grabbed their guns and went running along the causeway to help their hard-pressed companions. Nameless spurred his horse along that other way he knew, and Jeannie followed close behind him. It was a treacherous trail, and several times their horses slipped in the soft earth and they nearly came off. The low trees were a hazard, too, and they had to ride low over their horses' necks to avoid being swept off.

But they made good speed, and the gunfire behind them faded away until they could hardly hear it. That meant that they must be very nearly out of the swamp by now.

They were coming to the firmer ground, where the trees grew to greater heights and were closer together. There was high vegetation hereabouts, and Nameless looked at it with distrust. This was ideal country for ambush, he knew. But there was no time for precautions. He had to trust to luck and hope the way was clear. He had a hunch it would be . . .

A hand snatched out from a bush and grabbed his startled horse by the bridle rein. A leaping form burst through the screen of green and grappled with him. Jeannie screamed behind him.

Startled, Nameless saw hands reaching up to him on all sides. He saw faces that hadn't been there a second before — and there seemed to be dozens of them.

He had ridden right into an ambush!

He fought savagely, trying to spur his horse through them, and all the while Jeannie was screaming behind him, as if she too was in the grip of their enemies.

Then Nameless found himself dragged from the saddle and, still fighting, hurled to the ground. Even then he wouldn't give in, and lashed out, and then someone took a crack at him on the head with a stick — or it might have been the butt end of a rifle.

The fight was over.

The next thing Nameless knew, someone was dragging the bandages from his face.

A rough voice was growling: 'Let's have a look at this guy's face. He sure was a tiger in that fight!'

Nameless's eyes flickered open just as the bandages were torn away to reveal his face. He saw a heavily-moustached man bending over him. There was a startled expression on the man's face.

Nameless found a name on the end of his tongue. 'Ben Ryan!' He exclaimed. And then he put his hand to his head. He had remembered a name connected with this face, but the mists of oblivion still clung to his memory.

Ben Ryan exclaimed: 'Rhett Davidson! What on earth are you doin' in this get-up?'

Ben looked bewildered. 'We were told we were up agen a desperate lot of outlaw Rebels. You ain't no outlaw,' Ben exclaimed with certainty.

Jeannie had been dragged up, and

now as Ben helped Nameless to his feet she ran over to him, her eyes wondering.

'They know me,' Nameless said to her, and he was still bewildered, still dizzy from the effects of that blow. 'I'm — I'm Rhett Davidson.' Again his hand went to his head. 'I don't know more than that except I recognised Ben Ryan on sight.'

Jeannie wheeled on that grey-haired, kindly-looking man, with the pressing throng of men behind him. Rough-looking men, but not rough in the way that Reuben Slatt's men were.

'You know — Rhett?' The name came unfamiliarly to her lips. 'Who is he? What is his past? You see, he doesn't know anything about himself. Something happened some time ago and he's without his memory.'

Ben Ryan smiled at the earnestness of this lovely girl. Perhaps already he understood the relationship between them, and the need for a knowledge of Rhett Davidson's past.

'Rhett was a surveyor on the railroad construction job when we built the line out yonder. And a mighty good surveyor, too. I reckon we need you back, Rhett, now we're opening up the line again.'

Jeannie and the man who had been known as Nameless were standing together now, staring at those faces before them that were suddenly friendly. It was all so bewildering, they couldn't understand it. And yet it was so reassuring. But there was an important thing that a woman had to know.

Jeannie spoke. The words tumbled from her mouth before she really knew what she was saying, before she realised how she was giving herself away.

'Mr. Ryan, has Rhett any — any past?' She stumbled over the words. 'I mean, has Rhett a sweetheart or a wife that you know of?'

Ben Ryan looked from one to the other, and saw the almost pleading looks in those eyes that watched him as if trying to divine the answer.

He scratched his head and then said slowly: 'Wal, I can't tell a lie.' Their hearts sank. 'I reckon Rhett had dozens of gals — but no wife. Miss, you take a warnin' from an old man. He's a goldarn, no-good, flighty man! You have nothing to do with him!'

The relief was so enormous that though both laughed at the older man's badinage, neither moved even to look at each other. They didn't need to. Their future was made now, even if the past was never revealed. Rhett Davidson was a free man and that was how Jeannie McNay wanted it.

But that wasn't the end of everything. Ben Ryan pointed that out. His voice was stern, though mystified.

'We were called in by the marshal of Stampede. He told us there was a bunch of Rebs who had turned outlaw and were terrorising the district. I didn't expect to find you among 'em, Rhett. You weren't ever a fellar to get across with the law in the old days.'

‘I’m not now,’ Rhett Davidson said grimly, and swiftly he explained what had happened.

‘You’re on the wrong side, Ben. And all you men,’ he said, and there was an angry growl from those railroad workers pressing round to hear his words. Men didn’t like to follow false leaders, and now their anger was directed against the marshal who had Reuben Slatt and his gang for deputies.

Rhett said: ‘I’m going to give you advice, Ben. I reckon you ought to stop this fight, an’ force an enquiry. A proper enquiry would show that the law in these parts is in the hands of a bunch of outlaws. Surely you’ve heard of the exploits of Reuben Slatt?’

Ben Ryan’s face was grim. He nodded. He’d heard of Reuben Slatt. His mind was made up.

‘We don’t fight alongside that rabble, not knowingly. I’m going to pull out my men until we know the truth of this matter!’

But Rhett Davidson had got a plan

already forming in his mind. He knew things would be difficult for his followers, penned in the swamps behind him.

'Ben, you get on Jeannie's hoss! Jeannie can stay with your men for protection. They can go back up the pathway and let my Rebs know that they're on their side. Jeannie can help them in that.

'But you an' me are goin' to ride round the swamp and take Slatt's men in the rear.' That was the plan in his mind. Ben Ryan could shout to his men to capture a surprised Reuben Slatt and his gang. That would solve all their problems beautifully . . .

They mounted and went riding like furies out through the woodland and around that mighty quagmire. It took them half an hour to come to where they could see and hear the battle raging. The Rebels had been forced way back into the swamp now, and Ben and Rhett came riding along the causeway a good distance before they came upon their men. Ben was standing in his stirrups, shouting. His men, crouching behind cover, saw him and paused in their firing to listen to him.

He shouted to them to take the Reuben Slatt men prisoners. They must not fire again upon the Rebels.

It was a bewildering turn of events for the railroad workers, but Ben Ryan was their chief and a man to obey. They went running up the causeway towards where Reuben Slatt and his men were driving the smaller Rebel force deeper into the swamps. But Reuben Slatt wasn't going to be taken easily. He, too, had heard what Ben Ryan had been shouting. He was warned.

There followed an incredible period of fighting in those swamps. It was hand-to-hand in places, and so mixed up that at times no one knew which side any one was on.

Bandaged Rebels fought alongside railroad workers in an attempt to subdue the Slatt gang.

There were little knots of fighting

men — groups of Slatt men surrounded and fighting desperately from behind the cover of trees that reared out of the causeway. And others of the Slatt gang were risking their lives by taking to unfamiliar trails that promised safety . . . and ended in the deepest of swamps.

Rhett Davidson fought savagely to get through to his Rebels. He found the other railroad workers had come in by the back pathway. His eyes looked for Jeannie. Instead he saw her brother running towards him, his bandages down around his chin, blood streaming from his head.

Rhett raced across towards him, his gun firing because he could see Slatt men struggling in the distance to escape through the swamp. He shouted: 'Where's Jeannie?'

And the McNay boy shouted back: 'They got her! I don't know how it happened. Three fellars suddenly came running across and grabbed her and used her as a shield to help 'em get away. They've taken to a path through the swamps. I never saw that path before.'

Rhett saw the boy drop on his knees as if the wound was severe. He hadn't time to stay with him. Jeannie was his consideration now. He ran over towards that other pathway indicated by the McNay boy. He saw tracks and followed them.

This was a trail new to him, and he wondered if it was a possible way out. Maybe whoever had captured Jeannie was following a trail made by old Eb on his hunting expeditions.

Half a mile along this treacherous trail, he saw a figure lying on the pathway.

The figure stirred and raised himself. It was Bully Tozer.

Rhett went and stood over him. Tozer looked up at him through blood-matted hair and began to stagger to his feet. He had been badly hurt.

Rhett had his guns out, but Tozer took no notice of them. He began to stagger along the pathway, following the soft, kicked-up earth that marked the passage of Skulach and companions.

Rhett grabbed his arm and savagely swung him round. 'What have you done with that gal?'

Tozer snarled and shook off that grip. Yet he made no attempt to turn on the man who had been nameless. Instead he staggered along that faintly defined pathway. It was as if Tozer had no time for Rhett — only thoughts in his bemused mind concerning his companions in front.

Rhett ran by his side. He realised that his quarry had found horses — perhaps strays. Panic rose within him. He must be falling behind in that race.

He shouted: 'Skulach . . . ' But got no farther.

That bloody face came snarling round. 'Him. I'll kill him! God in heaven, that's what I'm gonna do!'

It startled Rhett. This wasn't the old, faithful, long-suffering Tozer. He wanted to know what had happened.

Again he grabbed and pulled Tozer round. 'Come on, talk, blast you! What happened?'

'We found old Eb.' Tozer was panting and wanting to talk now, wanting to spill this bile of hatred out of his system. 'Eb was catchin' hosses an' tryin' to keep 'em from runnin' into the swamps an' becomin' 'gator food.'

'Was Slatt with you?'

'Yeah. Slatt grabbed the old man an said he'd cut out his tongue ef he didn't lead us out of the swamps. So Eb said he would. Eb had got two hosses only.' Tozer's smouldering eyes glowed with hatred under that shaggy, matted mop of hair, remembering. 'Slatt got up on one with the old man. That left one hoss atween three of us.'

Tozer began to walk along the pathway then, but he was still talking. Now he couldn't stop. There was a curious swelling agony in the man — he had been hurt in a way no one could have expected, and he seemed like a child crying in anguish. Almost he was crying.

'A hoss'll carry two at a pinch. But not three. I started to go for the cayuse.' He licked his lips and his pace quickened. 'Somethin' hit me on the side of my head an' I went down. I got to my feet. Johnny had the gal up on the saddle afore him. I couldn't believe it was Johnny who had hit me.

'I went across. I was sick from that blow an' didn't know what I was doin', I reckon. I remember lookin' up an' sayin': 'You can't take that gal an' leave your pard behind.''

'Then what happened?' Nameless's voice was soft.

'He hit me agen with his gun an' I went down. As I went out I heard him . . . laughin'.'

Rhett Davidson said: 'That Skulach's a damned treacherous snake — ' But Tozer interrupted him. The man's voice was curiously impassioned. Now he had to tell someone of this monstrous injustice.

'You don't know the half of it. All my life I have looked after Johnny. I've stood by him. I've fought for him. I've put up with his tempers an' insults — only to have this happen to me!'

'Why did you let him wipe his feet on you all these years?'

There was no sign of their quarry ahead. There wouldn't be, of course. The gap would be widening with every minute. With old Eb to lead them out of the quags and mounted on horses, he and Tozer didn't have a chance. He cursed Eb for turning up when he had.

Tozer halted, and now he seemed veritably to rock with agony. 'Why? Don't you know? Because he's my brother! Yeah, we had the same mother — different paw, that was all. An' I had to bring him up from a baby.'

Tozer looked insane. Rhett found himself touched, because he knew that the cause of it was grief. Tozer had loved that half-brother of his. It was curious, but it was true.

Tozer shouted now: 'He left me to

die because he wanted that gal. I meant nothin' to him after all, even after all I've done for him. But, blast it, I'm gonna kill him, brother or no brother!'

He started to reel onwards, a gun in his hand now. And Rhett knew he would do as he threatened . . .

A scream tore through the wisps of vapour that seemed perpetually to be rising from the stinking swamp. It was an unearthly scream, a scream such as no human throat could have produced. Both men went running madly forward.

The pathway was getting softer. They were sinking over their boot tops, and yet still the tracks led onwards. Moisture oozed with every stride they took.

The bushes petered out. There were no trees. Only swamp grasses, and green, slimy swamp.

And across from them, no more than fifty yards away, was a rising hillock that told them that beyond the bubbling, steaming mud was high land and dry ground — and safety.

They heard someone come running out from the last of those bushes. Their guns turned.

It was Jeannie. Eb was sitting on his heels, looking with mild interest at the swamp. Things were moving. A horse, blackened with mud, came staggering out by some bushes to their left. Eb's old voice quavered: 'That beast sure was lucky. But it ain't too bad here. Not too bad. I reckon they had jest a chance.'

Jeannie was clinging to Rhett. She was sobbing. Tozer was shambling to the water's edge, more like a savage beast than a man.

Rhett whispered: 'Thank God you're safe! What happened?'

'Eb led them into a trap. He got them here, then said all they had to do was get across that bit of swamp and they'd be right out of the quags. He said they might make it if their horses weren't overloaded.' She looked across at the old man and whispered: 'There's more cunning in Eb than I thought.'

'They let you down?'

'They were in such a panic to save their skins they threw us right off the horses. They thought you might be right behind on other horses. Skulach was in terror at the thought of meeting Tozer again.'

Her horror-widened eyes were staring beyond him. He couldn't understand what she was looking at. Just something moving on the mud over by that dry land. His head turned sharply. In the distant grasses there was violent movement, as of great beasts threshing about.

Swiftly he asked: 'What happened to them?'

Eb answered. His finger pointed towards the disturbance in the grasses. ''gators,' he announced without emotion. 'Reuben Slatt's hoss found a deep hole, I reckon, an' went right under. Mebbe you heered its scream. I figger 'gators got at it afore it went under.'

Then the 'gators must have got Slatt, too. They'd be fighting over him right

now. His grip tightened on Jeannie. She was still watching that other movement over by dry land. It was coming out of the mud.

He heard her say: 'That's . . . Johnny Skulach. He's going to make it!' And there was gladness in her voice, as if she couldn't wish such a horrible death even for such a worthless creature.

Tozer's thick voice floated back: 'That's Johnny, huh?'

They saw him crawling out of the mire, towards the inevitable green fringe of rushes. He was like some long, black serpent, unrecognisable at that distance. They heard his voice. It was sobbing but there was hysterical triumph in it. Skulach had come through hell, but now he was sure he had won.

Tozer had his gun up. Eb saw it first and said: 'Them that live by the gun shall die by the gun.' But he was an old man and made no move to interfere.

Rhett saw it then, but knew he was too late to do anything. Those sights were on Skulach. An ounce more pressure and the man would die.

Skulach turned on his side, hands gripping that green swamp vegetation. He must have looked back then and seen the bloody figure of his half-brother with that gun pointing at him. They heard him moan, his cowardly soul in terror again.

For what seemed an age but could only have been a few seconds, those two hating brothers looked across that swamp at each other.

And then Tozer slowly lowered his gun and turned away. They saw his head slump to his chest as if the heart and strength had gone out of him. Then he raised his eyes to theirs and there seemed apology in them. As if he was ashamed of his weakness.

'Doggone it,' they heard him say. 'I was crazy 'bout that kid. The only relative I have in the world. Gosh a'mighty, I couldn't hurt him . . . '

Jeannie was sobbing. 'You're not bad. Not bad at all — '

Rhett hurled her away. He went

bounding across towards Tozer. Eb had seen the danger, too. Eb was pointing again across the swamp. 'He's pullin' a gun!' he shouted.

That gun was up, pointing across the swamp. Pointing straight at Tozer.

Tozer had given his half-brother his life. Now, some distorted thought process made Skulach want to shoot him when his back was turned.

That gun never fired. Skulach went mad. They saw the gun fall from his hand, saw him clamber out among the reeds and go running wildly in circles. He was holding his hand. His screams were awful to hear. They lost sight of him, but continued to hear his screams for a long time.

Something moved on the loose water that surfaced the swamp mud. Something small. They could see an arrow-shaped moving wave.

Eb sighed. 'Must have put his hand on a water moccasin. Blamed things in always in them reeds.' He rubbed his cheek reflectively. 'Guess he won't be able to stand the pisen like me. He'll stop screamin' soon.'

They got the muddy, trembling horse and began to walk back along the trail. Rhett called: 'You, Tozer, come with us. I'll do what I can to help you.'

Tozer wasn't all that bad, as Jeannie said. The man shambled behind them, not caring what happened to him, all the same. Johnny — the baby Johnny he had looked after — was dying. Soon he would be dead. A light would go out in Tozer's life. Maybe the only light.

The fighting was over, back by Eb's camp. They rested and attended to each other's wounds and then began the long trek out. With them were a couple of dozen sullen prisoners.

Ben Ryan rode with them into Stampede. The horrors of that experience within the swamps were fading in their minds. Jeannie and Rhett Davidson were holding hands as they rode, their thoughts about themselves and their future.

So Ben uttered a dry cough and said:

'I need you on the track, Rhett. You comin' back?'

'I sure am.' The man who had been Nameless turned a laughing face towards him. 'Don't you see, I'll be needin' a pay packet to keep a wife soon.'

Jeannie was laughing. And then Ben said: 'Rhett, which side did you fight on in the war? Yank or Reb?'

'You don't know?' Again Rhett was looking back. Ben shook his head. 'Then I hope I never know!'

His hand waved to embrace his Rebel friends. 'I'd sure hate to find I'd been wastin' my time fightin' guys as fine as them.'

THE END